## MAN AND BEAST

The shooting probably had the animal pretty spooked to start with. Now it let out a shrill whinny of fear and reared up on its hind legs, pawing frantically at the air with its front hooves.

One of those hooves smacked hard into Fargo's left shoulder and knocked him back a step. His left arm went numb. At the same time, with strength born of desperation, the bushwhacker swung a knobby fist that connected solidly with Fargo's jaw. For a second, sky-rockets went off behind the Trailsman's eyes and blinded him.

Fargo's vision recovered in time for him to see a heavy-bladed knife slicing toward his face. . . .

# THE
# TRAILSMAN

### #325

# SEMINOLE
# SHOWDOWN

### by

## Jon Sharpe

A SIGNET BOOK

SIGNET
Published by New American Library, a division of
Penguin Group (USA) Inc., 375 Hudson Street,
New York, New York 10014, USA
Penguin Group (Canada), 90 Eglinton Avenue East, Suite 700, Toronto,
Ontario M4P 2Y3, Canada (a division of Pearson Penguin Canada Inc.)
Penguin Books Ltd., 80 Strand, London WC2R 0RL, England
Penguin Ireland, 25 St. Stephen's Green, Dublin 2,
Ireland (a division of Penguin Books Ltd.)
Penguin Group (Australia), 250 Camberwell Road, Camberwell, Victoria 3124,
Australia (a division of Pearson Australia Group Pty. Ltd.)
Penguin Books India Pvt. Ltd., 11 Community Centre, Panchsheel Park,
New Delhi - 110 017, India
Penguin Group (NZ), 67 Apollo Drive, Rosedale, North Shore 0632,
New Zealand (a division of Pearson New Zealand Ltd.)
Penguin Books (South Africa) (Pty.) Ltd., 24 Sturdee Avenue,
Rosebank, Johannesburg 2196, South Africa

Penguin Books Ltd., Registered Offices:
80 Strand, London WC2R 0RL, England

First published by Signet, an imprint of New American Library,
a division of Penguin Group (USA) Inc.

First Printing, November 2008
10  9  8  7  6  5  4  3  2  1

The first chapter of this book previously appeared in *California Crackdown*,
the three hundred twenty-fourth volume in this series.

PUBLISHER'S NOTE

This is a work of fiction. Names, characters, places, and incidents either are
the product of the author's imagination or are used fictitiously, and any resem-
blance to actual persons, living or dead, business establishments, events, or
locales is entirely coincidental.

The publisher does not have any control over and does not assume any
responsibility for author or third-party Web sites or their content.

If you purchased this book without a cover you should be aware that this
book is stolen property. It was reported as "unsold and destroyed" to the
publisher and neither the author nor the publisher has received any payment
for this "stripped book."

The scanning, uploading, and distribution of this book via the Internet or via
any other means without the permission of the publisher is illegal and punish-
able by law. Please purchase only authorized electronic editions, and do not
participate in or encourage electronic piracy of copyrighted materials. Your
support of the author's rights is appreciated.

# The Trailsman

Beginnings . . . they bend the tree and they mark the man. Skye Fargo was born when he was eighteen. Terror was his midwife, vengeance his first cry. Killing spawned Skye Fargo, ruthless, cold-blooded murder. Out of the acrid smoke of gunpowder still hanging in the air, he rose, cried out a promise never forgotten.

The Trailsman they began to call him all across the West: searcher, scout, hunter, the man who could see where others only looked, his skills for hire but not his soul, the man who lived each day to the fullest, yet trailed each tomorrow. Skye Fargo, the Trailsman, the seeker who could take the wildness of a land and the wanting of a woman and make them his own.

*Indian Territory, 1860—where a trail of tears
leads Skye Fargo into a showdown with deadly danger.*

# 1

"Don't move, mister, or I'll blow your damn brains out."

The big man in buckskins stood absolutely still. A touch of amusement lurked in his lake blue eyes as he asked, "What about my hands? Do you want me to put my hands up?"

"Uh . . . yeah, that'd be good, I reckon. Put your hands up."

Skye Fargo lifted his hands to shoulder level. A faint smile tugged at the corners of his wide mouth, nestled in the close-cropped dark beard. But he was wary at the same time, because even though he could tell from the voice that the person who had threatened him was undoubtedly young and probably inexperienced, a bullet fired by such a person could still take his life.

"You want to be careful with that gun, whatever it is," Fargo advised. "Don't let your finger rest on the trigger, or you're liable to shoot before you really mean to. And I don't think either of us wants that."

"You just let me worry about when I shoot. Who the hell are you, anyway?"

"A friend," Fargo answered. "I'm looking for Billy Buzzard."

That brought a sharply indrawn breath from the youngster behind him. "You're a friend of Billy's?"

"That's right. We rode together a while back, doing some scouting for the army."

"Oh, my God. You're him. You're the Trailsman."

Fargo had to grin at the tone of awe in the kid's voice. That was one of the advantages—or drawbacks, depending on how you wanted to look at it—of having a reputation.

"Some call me that," he admitted. "But my name is Skye Fargo."

"You wouldn't be lyin' to me?"

"Nope."

"Well, then, I, uh, I reckon you can put your hands down, Mr. Fargo. I'm sorry I pointed this here—"

The sudden roar of a shot drowned out whatever the boy had been about to say.

Fargo felt as much as heard the wind rip of the bullet's passage close beside his right ear. He whirled around, thinking that the boy had accidentally pulled the trigger, just as Fargo had warned him he might.

He caught a glimpse of the youngster's face, though, which looked even more surprised than Fargo expected, and the next second another shot blasted somewhere nearby. A narrow branch leaped from a tree, cut off by the bullet.

Fargo lunged at the kid, knocking him off his feet and sending the boy's rifle flying. He rolled next to a deadfall and shoved the boy against it.

"Stay here, and keep your head down!" he ordered. A third shot sounded, knocking bark off the trunk of the fallen tree. That shot allowed Fargo to pinpoint the source of the ambush, because he saw powder smoke spurt from some brush atop a low bluff about twenty yards away.

Fargo's Henry rifle rode in a saddle sheath strapped to the magnificent black-and-white Ovaro stallion he'd left a short distance back up the gulch. Armed with

2

only a heavy Colt revolver, Fargo knew he'd have to get closer to the bushwhacker to do any good with the handgun. He crawled along the deadfall, keeping the thick trunk between him and the rifleman on the bluff.

He had expected trouble as soon as he realized a short time earlier that someone was following him as he rode through these rugged, thickly wooded hills. Whoever was on his trail, though, made so much racket that Fargo had soon decided it couldn't be anybody too well versed in the ways of the frontier. Growing impatient with being the prey instead of the hunter, he had dismounted and started up a rocky defile on foot, in hopes of drawing his pursuer in after him.

The trick had worked, sort of. Fargo had figured to get the drop on whoever was trailing him and find out what was going on. He wasn't surprised to discover it was a kid, a boy about sixteen from the looks of him.

But then somebody else had opened fire on both of them, and now Fargo had to deal with that problem.

He reached the end of the log and took off his wide-brimmed brown hat, setting it aside for the moment. Carefully, he edged his head around the log and peered up at the bluff. No more shots had sounded, and the brush didn't move or rustle. Fargo's instincts told him that the bushwhacker was still up there, though.

The man was probably crouched in the brush with his sights lined on the deadfall, just waiting for any sign of movement. That tension would have stretched his nerves taut by now. A grim smile touched Fargo's mouth. He'd give the son of a bitch something to shoot at.

He picked up his hat and sailed it at the bluff.

Sure enough, a shot erupted from the brush. But it

was aimed wildly at the flying hat, not at Fargo, who powered to his feet and sprinted toward the bluff. He triggered a couple of rounds in the direction of the bushwhacker, not worrying about hitting anything, just trying to come close enough to make the varmint duck instinctively for cover. That gave Fargo time to reach the base of the bluff.

From that angle, the rifleman couldn't draw a bead on Fargo, who holstered his Colt and started climbing. He used rocks and roots that protruded from the earth as handholds and footholds, and he needed only seconds to scale the dozen or so feet to the top of the bluff. He rolled over the edge and came to a stop on his belly, listening intently.

The shots would have scared away all the birds and small animals in the area, so when the Trailsman's keen ears picked up a faint rustling, he knew the bushwhacker had to be the one causing it. The man was trying to work his way closer to the edge of the bluff, maybe in hopes of being able to fire down at Fargo.

Too late for that. Fargo was already at the top, and he came up on one knee and drew his gun in the same motion as a roughly dressed man pushed some branches aside and stepped into view, clutching a rifle.

The man let out a surprised yelp at the sight of Fargo and jerked his weapon in the direction of the Trailsman. Fargo fired before the bushwhacker could get off a shot.

However, the man had turned enough so that Fargo's bullet slammed into the stock of the rifle he held, shattering it and knocking the gun out of the man's hand. He shouted in pain and whipped around to plunge back into the brush before Fargo could ear back the Colt's hammer and fire again.

Fargo surged to his feet and went after the man, holstering his gun again as he did so. Branches clawed

*4*

at him as he crashed through the brush. He could hear his quarry fleeing madly in front of him. The man was only a few steps ahead of Fargo when he broke out into the open again and lunged toward a horse tethered to a sapling.

The bushwhacker jerked the reins free, got a foot in the stirrup, and had started to swing up into the saddle when Fargo launched a flying tackle at him. He crashed into the bushwhacker and both men collided with the horse's flank.

The shooting probably had the animal pretty spooked to start with. Now it let out a shrill whinny of fear and reared up on its hind legs, pawing frantically at the air with its front hooves.

One of those hooves smacked hard into Fargo's left shoulder and knocked him back a step. His left arm went numb. At the same time, with strength born of desperation, the bushwhacker swung a knobby fist that connected solidly with Fargo's jaw. For a second, skyrockets went off behind the Trailsman's eyes and blinded him.

Fargo's vision recovered in time for him to see a heavy-bladed knife slicing toward his face. He ducked under the slashing attack, lowered his head, and butted his opponent in the belly. The man's breath *whoosh*ed out of his lungs as he doubled up and went over backward.

Fargo leaped after him in an effort to pin the man to the ground, but the hombre threw a booted foot up in time to kick Fargo in the stomach with it and send him falling off to the side.

Now they were both out of breath. Fargo rolled over and came up on his knees in time to see the bushwhacker grab a flapping stirrup on the skittish horse and use it to pull himself to his feet. The man still had hold of the knife. He flung it at Fargo, forcing the Trailsman to dive to the side to avoid the spinning blade.

That gave the bushwhacker time enough to haul himself into the saddle and kick the horse's flanks. He kept kicking as the horse broke into a gallop.

Fargo pushed himself up and palmed the Colt from its holster, but as he brought the revolver up, he hesitated. He could shoot the horse, or he could shoot the bushwhacker in the back, and both of those things went against the grain for him. Grimacing, he climbed to his feet as the bushwhacker and his mount disappeared into a grove of trees.

Fargo thought the chances of the varmint doubling back for another try were pretty slim. Once the initial attempt on Fargo's life had gone sour, the rifleman seemed to want nothing more than to get away.

Or maybe the man hadn't been trying to kill him at all, Fargo thought suddenly, at least not at first.

That kid had been down there, too, and the shots had come just about as close to him as they had to Fargo.

It was time for him to see if he could find out what in blazes this was all about, Fargo told himself.

First things first. He reloaded the Colt, then slipped it back into leather. Then he went back to the spot where he had shot the rifle out of the bushwhacker's hands and picked up the weapon with its shattered stock. There might be something unusual about it that would point him toward the owner, he thought.

The rifle had nothing distinctive about it, however. It was a Henry much like the one Fargo owned, but not as well cared for. And now, of course, it had a broken stock. A gunsmith could replace that, so Fargo took it with him.

He found a place where the bluff's slope was gentle

enough for him to be able to descend without having to climb down. As he walked toward the deadfall, he called, "All right, son, it's safe for you to come out now. Whoever that hombre was and whichever one of us he was after, he's gone now."

No answer came from behind the log. Fargo frowned and put his right hand on the butt of his Colt, carrying the broken rifle in his left as he approached. He looked over the rotting log.

The kid was gone.

At least there were no bloodstains on the ground to indicate that any of the shots had hit the youngster. He probably had a horse somewhere nearby, and as soon as he'd been able to tell that the fracas between Fargo and the bushwhacker had moved away from the edge of the bluff, more than likely he'd run down the gulch to find his mount and light a shuck out of here.

Clearly, though, the boy knew Billy Buzzard. His reaction when Fargo had mentioned the name had been one of familiarity. And he had recognized Fargo's name, too, which in all likelihood meant that Billy had told the youngster about him. Fargo had a hunch that if he went on to Billy's place, he might meet up with that kid again.

And if he did, he intended to get some answers.

Then again, he told himself as he whistled for the Ovaro, he had a few questions for Billy Buzzard, too.

The stallion trotted up the gulch toward him. Fargo had left the reins looped around the saddlehorn, preferring that the Ovaro be free to move around in case of trouble, rather than be tied up somewhere. The big black-and-white horse tossed his head angrily as he came up to Fargo, as if telling the Trailsman that he had heard the shots and didn't cotton to missing out on the action.

"Take it easy," Fargo told the stallion as he tied the broken rifle onto the back of the saddle. "Chances are there'll be more trouble, plenty for both of us."

No truer words were ever spoken, he thought as he retrieved his hat, which the bushwhacker's hurried shot had missed, and settled it on his head. One thing Fargo's adventurous career had taught him was that trouble was never long in coming. . . .

Skye Fargo had been in Wichita, Kansas, when the letter from Billy Buzzard caught up with him. It didn't amount to much—Billy never had been a long-winded cuss—just said his family needed help and asked if Fargo could come to Indian Territory. Since Billy had once used his own body to stop an arrow meant for the Trailsman, Fargo had saddled up the Ovaro and ridden south.

Billy Buzzard was a Seminole. Fargo didn't know his true name, only the one by which white men knew him. Born in Florida, as a youngster Billy had been uprooted along with the rest of his people and taken to Indian Territory as part of the forced migration known to the Indians as the Trail of Tears.

The so-called Five Civilized Tribes—Cherokee, Choctaw, Chickasaw, Creek, and Seminole—were now settled here. Although far from their original homelands, they were doing the best they could to establish new lives for themselves. They lived up to the "civilized" designation, setting up their own governments and schools and policing themselves for the most part, although the U.S. Army, headquartered at Fort Gibson, had the final responsibility for maintaining order in Indian Territory.

The Seminoles were the smallest tribe of the five, and in the minds of some, were also the most primitive and warlike. Under the leadership of their chief Osceola, they had fought long and hard against the army in Florida before finally being conquered.

Billy Buzzard had been too young for those campaigns, and so he bore no real animosity or distrust toward the whites. His restless nature had led him to leave his people for a few years, and during that time he had worked as a scout for the army on the high plains of Kansas, Nebraska, and Colorado Territory, helping the bluecoats fight the Cheyenne, the Pawnee, and the Kiowa. He had met Fargo during that part of his life.

The time had come when Billy wanted to return to his family in Indian Territory, and Fargo hadn't seen him since then, hadn't even heard from him until the arrival of the crudely printed letter. Billy had learned to write since Fargo had known him; either that or he had gotten somebody to write the letter for him.

The letter had been mailed from Fort Gibson, but Fargo knew the Seminole Nation was a good distance southwest of the fort, a fairly small area carved out between the Creek and Chickasaw reservations. That was where he would find Billy Buzzard, a region of fairly level terrain broken up by stretches of wooded hills and ridges. It was decent farmland, Billy had told Fargo, when the rains didn't come too often and turn it into a bog. The numerous rivers and creeks in the area had a tendency toward flooding.

The farm belonging to Billy's family lay near one of those streams, Jumper Creek, not far north of the south fork of the Canadian River. Fargo knew he was getting close. He had replenished his supplies at Fort Gibson, and now they were running low.

Of course, he wasn't worried about going hungry if he didn't reach his destination today. Small game abounded in this region, and plenty of edible plants grew here as well.

9

But after the run-in with the kid, and then the ambush attempt, his gut told him that Billy had been right about the trouble plaguing his family. Fargo wanted to help his old friend if he could.

He came to a stream he was pretty sure was Jumper Creek and followed it. Tendrils of smoke rose here and there in the distance, twisting through the late-afternoon sky. Fargo figured the smoke came from the chimneys of Seminole cabins.

A narrow road that was little more than a trail crossed the creek on a rickety wooden bridge up ahead. Fargo reached the bridge just as a wagon approached it along the road from the north. He reined in to let the wagon cross first, but the driver hauled back on the lines and brought the vehicle to a stop.

Fargo's lake blue eyes narrowed in surprise as he saw that despite the rough work clothes and the shapeless hat crammed down on thick dark hair, the driver was a woman. The breasts that swelled proudly under the homespun fabric of her shirt were unmistakable proof of that.

Fargo was about to nod and say howdy when the woman reached down to the floorboard at her feet and picked up a shotgun. She pulled back the hammers, pointed it at him, and said, "If you try to come near me, mister, I'll blow you in half. I swear I will."

She spoke in a bold, defiant voice, but it held an undertone of fear, too. Folks sure were jumpy around here, Fargo thought. They kept pointing guns at him. First the kid, and now this woman.

Staying right where he was and keeping his hands in plain sight, Fargo said, "I'm not looking for any trouble, ma'am. So I'd sure be obliged if you'd lower those hammers and point that scattergun somewhere else."

She snorted in disbelief. "Of course you're not looking for trouble," she snapped. "A white man in the

**10**

middle of the Seminole Nation. What *are* you looking for, then?"

"Not what," Fargo said. "Who. Billy Buzzard, to be precise."

That surprised her. "Billy—" she started to exclaim. "You mean At-loo-sha?"

Fargo shook his head. "Sorry. I don't know his Seminole name, only what he was called when he was working as a scout for the cavalry."

She didn't take the shotgun's hammers off cock, but she did lower the barrels slightly. "You knew At-loo-sha when he lived with the white men?"

"That's right."

"Is your name Fargo?"

He smiled. "Right again. I'd be obliged if maybe folks would start asking me what my name is *before* they go to pointing guns at me."

She ignored that and said, "Thank the Lord. At-loo-sha—Billy as you call him—said that you would come to help us." She finally lowered the hammers and replaced the shotgun on the floorboard. "Have you been to his house yet?"

"Nope. I just got to these parts earlier this afternoon."

"I'm on my way there now. Come with me."

"I'd be glad to."

She picked up the reins and slapped them against the backs of the mules pulling the wagon. The wheels clattered across the bridge. Fargo followed her on the Ovaro, and once they were south of the creek, he brought the stallion up alongside the wagon.

"Just to complete the introduction, I'm Skye Fargo," he told her as they followed the narrow path.

"Echo McNally."

Fargo had to smile. "That's a mighty pretty name. It suits you."

She returned the smile, a little reluctantly, Fargo thought. "Thank you." She didn't look at him but kept her attention focused on the mule team instead.

That gave him a chance to study her profile, which was clean and strong and quite attractive. The smooth, reddish brown skin was a bit lighter than that of most Indians, showing that she was of mixed blood. Not surprising, since the Seminoles had freely intermarried with white outlaws and runaway slaves who had fled to the swamps in Florida. Even earlier, French and Spanish explorers had contributed their bloodlines to the Seminoles, as well as pirates of all races. It was a rich heritage, and Echo McNally looked like she might have a little of all those backgrounds in her.

Her name didn't surprise Fargo, either. Many members of the Five Civilized Tribes had taken "white" names. Some had never even been given traditional tribal names, especially the ones born since the removal to Indian Territory.

Echo was in her early twenties, Fargo judged. He asked, "Are you related to Billy? Or just his friend?"

"His family and my family have been friends for many years," she answered. "Since before our people were brought here."

Fargo nodded, wondering if maybe Billy and Echo were more than friends. He would inquire of Billy about that later on, though. He didn't want to embarrass the young woman.

"Mind if I ask you something else?"

"I suppose not."

"Why is everybody so jumpy around here? Billy wrote to me and told me he needed my help with some trouble, but he didn't explain what it was."

"I know." Echo glanced over at Fargo. "I wrote the letter for him."

"Then I'm betting you can tell me what's going on."

"Billy might prefer to do that himself," she hedged.

"Maybe. But the sooner I know what's wrong, the sooner I can start figuring out what to do about it."

"You seem very confident that you can help us."

Fargo shrugged. "I'm very confident that I can do my best to help you. That's exactly what I intend to do."

She thought about it for a couple of seconds longer before she nodded and said, "All right. People have been disappearing from around here, and no one knows what's happening to them. Women, specifically. *Young* women."

Fargo frowned. "And you're out driving around the countryside by yourself? I see why you brought along a shotgun."

"I know how to use it, too," she said with a touch of defiance.

"I'll bet you do. I'm still not sure it's a good idea for you to be out here."

"Nobody's going to stop me from going where I want to go and doing what I want to do." Now her voice was hot with anger. "I can take care of myself, no matter what—"

She stopped short, and Fargo wondered if she'd been about to say, "no matter what Billy says."

"Anyway," Echo resumed after a moment, "more than a dozen girls have vanished over the past three months. I should say that they've been taken, because I'm certain they didn't go on their own, wherever they went."

"You can't know that for sure," Fargo pointed out. "Sometimes folks will run off without telling anybody, especially young ones. They argue with their parents, or they want to get married, or—"

"Not these girls," Echo interrupted. "They weren't the sort to do that. Besides, some of them were already happily married."

"It's hard to know exactly what somebody will do. People will fool you sometimes."

Echo shook her head stubbornly. Fargo didn't press the issue. She had to know more about it than he did, he reasoned, since she lived here and was acquainted with the people involved.

"Go on," he urged. "How did the girls disappear? They couldn't just vanish into thin air."

"At first, before people realized what was going on, they would be walking from one place to another and simply fail to arrive at their destination. Sometimes it would be one girl alone; sometimes two walking together. Then they began to disappear from the fields where they were working, or from their cabins when they were alone. By then people began to be afraid. Women were more closely guarded by their fathers or husbands. For a time no one vanished, and we hoped that whatever it was, it was over."

"But it wasn't," Fargo guessed.

Echo shook her head with a grim expression on her face. "It has started again. In the past week two young women have disappeared, including Wa-nee-sha . . . At-loo-sha's sister."

"Billy's sister?" Fargo said. "That's happened since he wrote me that letter, then. Or since you wrote it, I should say."

"Billy told me what to put down on the paper. They were his words. He said that no one could follow a trail as well as you, that if anyone could find the women who had disappeared, it was Skye Fargo. Now we have more reason than ever to hope that he was right about you, Mr. Fargo."

That was a heavy responsibility to put on a fella,

**14**

Fargo thought with a frown. Some of the missing women had been gone for weeks. Any trails they might have left would be so cold as to be almost impossible to follow.

But the disappearances had to be connected. Nothing else made any sense. So if he could find the women who had vanished the most recently, he might have at least a slim chance of finding the others, or finding out what had happened to them, anyway.

He didn't want to say as much to Echo, but there was a chance some of the women were dead. Whatever was happening to them, it couldn't be good.

Wanting to fill in more of the background, he asked, "Has anybody noticed any strangers in the area lately? Somebody who might be abducting those girls?"

Echo nodded. "People have seen groups of riders at night. No one knows who they are or what they want. Two men tried to follow their trail." She paused. "They never came back. But we think those strangers are white men, trying to conceal their identities by riding at night. That's why I was so suspicious of *you*."

And chances were, that explained why the kid had been following him earlier and then tried to capture him. The youngster must have thought that he had trapped one of the men responsible for all the trouble.

That might have explained the ambush, too . . . an overeager Seminole who believed he was taking a shot at somebody who had been kidnapping Seminole women . . . except for a couple of things. The boy was an Indian, and those bullets had come perilously close to him.

And the bushwhacker Fargo had tussled with had been white. He hadn't gotten a good look at the hombre, and it was true that some of the Seminoles with their mixed blood could pass for white . . . but that rifleman had had very fair, freckled skin and flaming red hair. Fargo doubted if there was a drop of Indian blood in his veins.

He and Echo had come about a mile from the bridge over Jumper Creek. She said, "The farm is just over that rise ahead of us. I'm sure Billy will be glad to see you."

"I'll be glad to see him," Fargo said with a smile. "I wouldn't be here today if it weren't for him. We got mixed up in a hot little skirmish with a Pawnee war party one time, and he wound up with an arrow in him that was meant for me."

"Really? He never told me about that. Is that why he limps?"

"Yeah. It stuck in his hip. The company surgeon had to cut it out, and the wound never healed up just right. The limp never slowed Billy down much, though." Fargo grinned. "I remember one time in Omaha—"

He stopped short as he realized that the story he'd been about to tell involved Billy Buzzard and not one, not two, but *three* soiled doves and wasn't even close to being fit for the ears of a lady.

"Yes, Mr. Fargo?" Echo said coolly. "Go on."

"Ah, maybe you'd better ask Billy about that." They had reached the top of the rise, and Fargo gestured at the log house that was visible a couple of hundred yards away. "That's the farm up there, I reckon."

"So it is," Echo said. She flicked the reins and called out to her mules, urging them to a faster pace. She and Fargo started down the gentle slope toward the farm.

But they hadn't gone very far when a volley of shots blasted out, shattering the late-afternoon stillness.

# 2

Fargo reined in sharply and leaned forward in the saddle, motioning for Echo to bring the wagon to a halt as he did so. The light had begun to fade because the sun was almost down to the horizon in the west, but the Trailsman's keen eyes made out puffs of powder smoke from some trees on the other side of the big, log farmhouse.

"Stay here," Fargo told Echo. "I'll ride down and see if I can give Billy and his folks a hand."

"I should come, too," she insisted. She gestured toward the scattergun at her feet. "I'm a good shot!"

"Those trees where the bushwhackers are holed up are too far away from the house for a greener to do any good," Fargo said, suppressing a surge of impatience at having to argue with her. "Blast it, just stay here!"

With that, he heeled the Ovaro into a gallop that carried man and horse down the slope. The stallion's hooves drummed against the ground.

Fargo guided the Ovaro with his knees as he slid the Henry from its sheath. The back of a galloping horse was no place for accuracy, but he brought the rifle to his shoulder and cranked off a few rounds toward the trees anyway, hoping to distract the hidden gunmen from their attack on the cabin. A moment later, the slope dropped down far enough so that he

17

could no longer see the trees because the cabin was in the way. But that meant the attackers couldn't see him, either.

Now, if only the folks forted up inside the cabin didn't take him for one of the varmints and open fire on him themselves. . . .

That didn't happen, and a moment later he brought the Ovaro to a skidding halt near a pole corral behind the house, which was large enough to have a back door, unlike smaller cabins that usually had only one entrance. Fargo vaulted out of the saddle and headed for the door at a run, carrying the repeating rifle.

Somebody must have seen him coming, because the door suddenly swung open. Fargo bounded to the porch and ducked through the door, which slammed shut behind him. Gloom surrounded him. No lamps or candles burned inside the house, and he found the shadows hard to penetrate as his eyes tried to adjust.

Those who were already inside the place could see better, as was demonstrated when someone called out, "Skye, you old horse thief! I thought it was you!"

Despite the fact that several years had passed, Fargo recognized Billy Buzzard's voice. He headed across the big main room toward the windows at the front. The defenders had pulled the shutters on those windows nearly closed, leaving only narrow slits through which to fire.

Those slits could let bullets in as well as out, though, and Fargo heard the high-pitched whine of a slug ricocheting from something inside the room. As he found a window no one was defending, he dropped to a knee, poked the Henry's barrel through the gap between the shutters, and said, "I should've known I'd find you up to your neck in trouble, Billy. It always had a way of finding you."

Billy laughed from where he crouched at a window

on the far side of the door. "You're a fine one to talk, Skye. I never saw a man who could attract more ruckuses than you."

Fargo fired toward the trees, which he could still see despite the gathering dusk. The shadows made the muzzle flashes under the trees more easily visible and gave him plenty of targets. At least a dozen men were out there, firing at the house.

That group of night riders Echo had mentioned? Fargo thought that was likely, but of course he couldn't know for sure that was who was attacking the farm.

He emptied the Henry at the trees, then turned and sat down with his back against the wall under the window as he reached into one of the pockets of his buckskins for a handful of fresh cartridges.

As he thumbed the rounds through the rifle's loading gate, he looked around the room. Three men were at the other windows. Billy Buzzard was the only one with a repeater; the other two men, one older and one younger than Billy, had old single-shot rifles.

Two women in the room as well, an older woman and a girl about fourteen. They were reloading for the men, who passed their empty rifles back and took freshly loaded weapons from the women.

As the younger man turned so that Fargo could see his face, he recognized the kid who had jumped him earlier in the gulch. That he was here came as no surprise to Fargo. He'd been halfway expecting as much.

Billy Buzzard could fill him in on everything that Echo McNally hadn't already told him, Fargo thought. Of course, before that could happen there was a little matter of surviving this attack on the farm. . . .

Fargo finished reloading the Henry and turned around to kneel at the window again. As he thrust the rifle's barrel through the gap between the shutters, he saw that the muzzle flashes in the trees had become more sporadic. He fired a couple of times, then lowered the Henry and said, "I think they're pulling out."

"Hold your fire!" Billy called to the others. "Skye's right. Those bastards are lightin' a shuck out of here!"

"Billy!" the old woman scolded. "Such language in front of the children!"

Billy grinned. "Sorry, Ma. When you spend much time around soldiers, you get in the habit of cussin'."

"Yes, and that's just one more reason you never should have left home," the woman said. "You're not going to learn anything worth knowing from white men." She glanced at Fargo. "No offense, Mr. Fargo."

"None taken," Fargo assured her with a smile of his own.

He leaned closer to the window and listened as the sound of a large group of horses came to his ears. The hoofbeats diminished, proving that the men who had attacked the farm were leaving.

Or at least their horses were, Fargo corrected himself. This could be a trick designed to draw Billy and his family out of the house and into the open.

"You'd better stay behind these sturdy log walls for a while, just to make sure they're really gone," he warned them.

Billy nodded in the gloom. "That's just what I was thinkin'." He had been kneeling at the window, but he stood up now, using his rifle to support him as he rose to his feet. He walked over to Fargo, limping on his right leg. He stuck out his hand, and Fargo grasped it.

"Good to see you again, Billy," Fargo said. "You look like you're doing well."

"As well as can be expected," Billy agreed. He

turned to wave a hand at the older couple. "You never met my folks, but you heard me talk about them."

Fargo nodded. "I sure did. It's an honor to meet you both."

The older man wore traditional Seminole garb: a shirt of faded red homespun that reached almost to his knees; a long, beaded sash that was looped around his shoulders, crossed over his chest, and tied around the waist for a belt; and buckskin leggings decorated with beadwork matching that on the sash. His iron gray hair hung loose around his head rather than being confined by a feathered turban such as many of the older Seminoles wore.

"I am Cam-at-so," he told Fargo as he shook hands. "My wife is Mary Ann," he added, confirming that the mixture of Seminole and white names was common, even within the same family.

Billy's mother wore a long gingham dress and had a striped shawl around her shoulders. Her hair was still dark, but her face showed her age. She gave Fargo a grave nod as he touched a finger to the brim of his hat and said, "Ma'am."

The boy Fargo had met earlier edged up to Billy and said, "I told you I saw him, Billy. I told you I met Skye Fargo!"

"Yeah, and you said the last you saw of him, somebody was trying to kill him," Billy said. "You shouldn't have run off and left him like that, Charley."

"But I wanted to let you know he was coming! You said if there was anybody in the world who could help us, it was the Trailsman!"

Echo had quoted Billy as saying pretty much the same thing. Billy must have built him up mighty big to these folks. Fargo didn't want to let them down.

"Skye, this little rapscallion is Charley McCloud,"

Billy said, continuing the introductions. "A fever carried away his ma a while back, and since his pa, uh, isn't around anymore, my folks sort of took him in to finish raising him."

"Hello, Charley," Fargo said.

"I'm sorry I ran off like that earlier," the youngster said. "Billy's right. I should have stayed to help you."

"That's all right," Fargo told him. "I made it out of that scrape with my hide intact."

"I want to hear about that," Billy said, "but first, meet my sister Daisy." He put his arm around the shoulders of the girl, who was beginning to blossom into beautiful young womanhood. Her expression was solemn beyond her years, though, and Fargo recalled what Echo had told him about Billy's sister vanishing. Echo must have meant another sister.

Fargo said, "Hello, Daisy." He looked at Billy. "I heard that you have another sister. . . ."

"Wa-nee-sha," Billy's mother said. She put her hands over her weathered face and began to weep.

Billy wore a grim expression as he said, "That's right. She's a few years older than Daisy here. Whoever's been grabbing girls from around here got her a few days ago, too." He frowned. "You know about that, Skye?"

"I've heard some about it."

"From who?"

"A lady I met on the way here named Echo McNally."

"Echo! She's here?"

"I left her and her wagon on the hill when we saw that the place was under attack," Fargo said with a vague wave toward the rear of the farmhouse. "I reckon I'd better go back and let her know it's safe to come down here—"

The dull, distant boom of a shotgun going off cut into his words.

Fargo swung toward the sound, an expression of alarm appearing on his bearded face. Taking the Henry with him, he broke into a run across the room. When he reached the back door, he flung it open and bounded down to the ground from the porch without using the steps. A whistle brought the Ovaro to him.

In the blink of an eye, Fargo was mounted and racing back to the spot where he had left Echo McNally. He didn't think she would use that scattergun without good reason, such as being in danger.

The sun had dropped completely below the horizon by now, and a soft gray mantle cloaked the landscape. Fargo could make out the wagon at the top of the hill, as well as hurried movement around it, but he couldn't tell for sure what was going on.

The shotgun's second barrel roared, adding more urgency to Fargo's already worried expression. He leaned forward over the stallion's neck and urged the horse on to greater speed. It was hard to be sure with the thunder of galloping hoofbeats in the air, but he thought he heard Echo scream.

The dash to the top of the rise took only moments, but it seemed longer than that to Fargo. He drew close enough to see Echo struggling in the grip of two men who were trying to drag her toward some waiting horses. Fargo whipped the Henry to his shoulder and fired two shots, aiming high enough so that there was no chance of the bullets hitting Echo.

The shots accomplished their goal anyway. The two men let go of her and turned to run as she slumped to the ground near the wagon. They reached their horses and threw themselves into the saddles as Fargo approached.

He let loose with two more shots, now that Echo was out of the line of fire, but both bullets missed. At least the two men showed no sign of injury as they fled. They frantically banged their feet against the flanks of their mounts and sent the horses galloping away.

Fargo wanted to go after them, but he couldn't tell how badly Echo was hurt, if at all. Checking on her condition took top priority. He hauled back on the Ovaro's reins and dropped out of the saddle while the big stallion was still moving. A couple of swift steps brought him to Echo's side.

The men had knocked her hat off and ripped one shoulder of her man's shirt during the struggle. Her eyes were closed. Fargo set the rifle on the ground and took hold of her shoulders, carefully raising her to a half-sitting position. Despite the fact that he had known her less than an hour, worry for her gnawed at him as he said, "Echo! Echo, can you hear me?"

He saw her eyelids flutter. She let out a low moan. Fargo ran his gaze along her body, looking for any sign of injuries. He kept his left arm around her shoulders and rested his right hand on her chest, seeking and finding the strong, steady beat of her heart.

"Mr. . . . Fargo?" she said groggily. "What are you . . . doing?"

Fargo realized that his hand rested halfway on the soft swell of her breast as he felt her heartbeat. He left it where it was as he said, "Just making sure that you're all right, Miss McNally."

"I . . . I'm fine," she said, with some of the customary crispness coming back into her voice. Fargo moved his hand away from her breast as he helped her sit up all the way. "Those men . . . ?"

"They're gone," Fargo said as he glanced in the direction the two men had fled. "They took off for the tall and uncut, and they weren't looking back. Did they hurt you?"

"No, I don't think they . . ." She shook her head. "No, I'm fine," she said more emphatically. "I may have a few bruises where they grabbed me and man-handled me, but nothing to worry about. They were armed, but I was the only one who got off a shot."

"Yeah, I heard both barrels of that greener go off. Did you hit either of them?"

"I don't think so," Echo said, and now she sounded disgusted. "I had a perfect chance to bring down two of the men who have been causing so much trouble around here, and I missed! I flinched when I pulled the trigger both times."

"Shooting a man's not as easy as it sounds," Fargo told her, his tone gentle. "Especially when you've never done anything like that before, which I reckon you haven't."

She shook her and said in a half whisper, "No, I haven't."

"Well, don't worry about it. You're all right, and that's the main thing."

She looked up at him. "What about At-loo-sha and his family?"

"They're all right, too," Fargo assured her. The sound of several horses coming up the hill made him turn his head and look over his shoulder. "In fact, here come a couple of them now."

Billy and Charley rode up hurriedly and reined in when they reached the wagon. "Echo!" Billy cried as he awkwardly flung himself down from the saddle while Fargo helped the young woman to her feet. "Are you all right?"

"I'm fine," she told him. "Those men didn't hurt me."

Billy threw his arms around her and hugged her.

"Thank God for that!" He looked at Fargo. "Could you tell who they were, Skye?"

Fargo shook his head. "I'm new in these parts, remember? They were just a pair of rough-looking hombres to me. What about you, Miss McNally? Did you get a good look at them?"

"I did, but I'd never seen them before," Echo said. "I couldn't even tell for sure if they were white or Indian . . . although they must have been white."

Fargo didn't think it was that much of a certainty. He understood why Echo would want to think that it couldn't be any of her own people kidnapping those girls and young women, but human predators often preyed on their own kind and always had, he figured, right from the dawn of history until now.

"Where'd the varmints go?" Charley asked from the back of his horse.

"They galloped off in that direction," Fargo said, pointing.

"I'll go see if I can find 'em," the youngster volunteered eagerly.

Billy let go of Echo and grabbed Charley's reins. "Oh, no, you won't! What do you reckon my ma would do to me if I let you go off and get yourself killed?"

"Aw, Billy! Somebody's got to stop those bastards and get Wa-nee-sha and all those other gals back!"

"Somebody's going to," Billy said with a grim nod. "Me and Mr. Fargo. Now, if you really want to help, Charley, climb down off that horse and drive Miss Echo's wagon on down to the house."

"I can drive my own wagon," Echo protested. She took a step toward the vehicle, then stopped short and swayed a little as if she'd gotten dizzy. Billy took hold of her arm to keep her from falling. "Guess I'm not as steady on my feet as I thought I was. One of those men hit me. . . ." She lifted a hand to her jaw.

"Let me see," Billy said. He cupped her chin in his hand and turned her head a little. "Blast it, it's getting too dark to see anything. Let's get you on down to the house."

"I guess that would be a good idea. That's where I was going, anyway, when I ran into Mr. Fargo."

It took them only a moment to get organized. Billy helped Echo onto the wagon seat while Charley tied his horse on at the back of the vehicle. Then Billy and Fargo mounted up and they all headed down the hill toward the farm.

"Is everyone all right at your place?" Echo asked, even though Fargo had already answered that question. Evidently she wanted to hear it from Billy, too. "Mr. Fargo and I saw that the farm was under attack when we rode up."

"Nobody was hit," Billy told her from horseback. "Charley and I were outside tending to a few last chores before dark when whoever it was opened up on us from the trees. The bullets came a mite too close for comfort, but we were able to scramble back inside before either of us got elected."

"Why would anybody try to kill you like that? Has this whole part of the territory gone mad?"

Fargo wondered the same thing himself. What he had seen and heard so far didn't seem to make a lot of sense. But that was probably because he couldn't see the whole picture yet, he told himself.

Maybe once he had talked more to Billy and his family, he would have a better understanding of what was going on around here.

The sharp tang of gun smoke had filled the air in the house when Fargo left. While some of that scent lingered, the much more pleasant smell of strong coffee now dominated. Someone had lit a lamp, too, casting a warm yellow glow over the main room. That light spilled out through the open door.

"Charley, take Miss McNally on inside," Fargo told the youngster. "Billy and I are going to have a look around and make sure those fellas who were here earlier are really gone."

"Let me come with you," Charley begged, but Billy shook his head.

"Do what Mr. Fargo tells you," he said. "He's the boss around here now, at least when it comes to fighting those kidnappers."

Grumbling, Charley helped still-dizzy Echo down from the wagon and held her arm as they went inside. Fargo and Billy rode toward the trees where the attackers had hidden earlier. They held their rifles ready for instant use.

"I reckon what you really wanted was a chance to talk to me alone, Skye. Ain't that right?"

"Partially," Fargo admitted. "I want to be sure none of those hombres are still skulking around, though."

"Good idea. I wouldn't put anything past 'em."

"Billy," Fargo said, "what the hell's going on around here?"

The former scout sighed. "I don't know what Echo told you already. . . ."

"That a dozen or more girls and young women have disappeared from around here in the past few months."

"That's true. And two men who went to look for them vanished, too."

"Yeah, she said something about that. You reckon they found more than they bargained for?"

"Damn right I do," Billy replied grimly. "I think those two fellas are lying in shallow graves right now . . . if they're lucky. More than likely the bastards left 'em for the crows and the coyotes."

Fargo thought his old friend was probably right about that. "Miss McNally mentioned something about a gang of night riders, too. . . ."

"Yeah. We've heard 'em, but nobody's gotten a good look at them. Everybody thinks they're the ones responsible for those girls disappearing. Let's face it, Skye—there's only one reason to be stealing gals like that. They're being held somewhere and being used as . . . as . . ."

Billy couldn't finish what he had started to say, and the strain in his voice reminded Fargo that one of Billy's own sisters was among the missing. He didn't want to think about the fate that might have befallen her.

"That's the first thing I thought of, too," Fargo said quietly, "but we don't know that's the case, Billy. There could be something else behind this."

Billy's voice was bitter and angry as he said, "I don't see what."

"That's what we've got to find out."

They had reached the trees. Cautiously, they rode into the shadows under the branches. Although a thin line of red remained on the western horizon, a reminder of the sun that had set, in these woods it was almost as dark as full night. Fargo brought the Ovaro to a halt and listened intently. He didn't hear anything out of the ordinary.

"They're gone," Billy said after a moment.

"Yeah," Fargo agreed. "I want to come out here in the morning when there's some good light and take a look around. One of them might have dropped something that could give us a clue who they are or what they want."

"You mean what they want other than me and my family dead?"

"Even if it's just that, there has to be a reason,"

Fargo pointed out. "I want to see if I can pick up the trail of those men who tried to grab Miss McNally, too."

"Yeah. Thanks for running them off, Skye. If anything happened to Echo, I don't know what I'd do."

Well, that answered the question of whether or not there was anything between Billy and Echo, Fargo thought. Billy was fiercely protective of her, like any man would be with a woman he cared about.

Just as well, Fargo told himself. If he was going to get to the bottom of this mess, he didn't need any distractions . . . even ones as pretty as Echo McNally.

They rode back to the house and circled around to the corral and barn in the back. From what Fargo had seen of the farm, it could have belonged to white settlers almost anywhere on the frontier. The Seminole were "civilized," all right . . . although Fargo had always believed it was a mite arrogant of folks to think of them that way when what they really meant was that the Civilized Tribes acted more like whites than they did like Indians. That didn't stop most people from looking down on them as redskins, either. Seemed to Fargo that in many ways Billy's people, along with the other tribes originally from the eastern woodlands, had gotten the short end of the stick all the way around.

It wasn't up to him to solve problems like that, however. He was more concerned with the night riders and kidnappers making life miserable for the folks who lived around here.

He and Billy unsaddled their horses and turned them into the corral. "I see you've still got that big Ovaro," Billy commented. "That stallion's a mighty fine horse."

"He's pulled me out of plenty of scrapes—that's

for sure," Fargo agreed as they walked toward the house.

"I'll come out later and see that he's got plenty of grain. I know not to get too close to him, though. I remember how he took a bite out of that sergeant's hide one day when the sarge got too pushy."

Fargo grinned. "Yeah, Sergeant Ferguson steered clear of him after that."

They went into the house and saw that the other members of the family, plus Echo McNally, were sitting around a big, rough-hewn table. Echo looked better now as she sipped at a cup of coffee, as if her dizziness had subsided. In the light of the lamp, Fargo could see that a bruise was beginning to form on her jaw, about halfway between her left ear and her chin. That was where one of the men she'd struggled with had clipped her with a punch.

"Those men are gone," Billy announced. "Skye and I took a good look around and didn't see any sign of them."

"Why would they attack us?" his father, Cam-at-so, asked. "We have no enemies. We have done nothing to injure anyone."

"Maybe they're after the farm," Fargo suggested as he accepted a cup of coffee from Billy's mother, Mary Ann. "Is there anything about it that would make it more valuable than the other farms around here?"

Billy shrugged. "Nothing that I can think of. Pa? How about you?"

Cam-at-so shook his head and said, "It is just a farm. The land is good for growing crops, but no better than that belonging to anyone else among our people."

"Well, there has to be some reason they jumped you this evening," Fargo said. "Maybe if we can find those missing girls, we'll find the answer to that question, too."

A worried frown creased Billy's forehead. "You'll try to pick up their trail, Skye?"

"First thing in the morning," Fargo promised.

"Now you must eat," Billy's mother said. "There is plenty for all. You, too, Echo."

"Thank you," the younger woman said, "but I really should be getting back home. I just wanted to drive over and see if you'd heard anything about Wa-nee-sha."

Cam-at-so shook his head sadly. "I wish we had. Perhaps soon."

"You're not driving back to your folks' place tonight," Billy said to Echo. "After what happened to you a little while ago? No way in—" He stopped short at his mother's glare of disapproval, then continued. "There's plenty of room here. You can spend the night and go home in the morning."

Mary Ann nodded and told Echo, "My son is right. You should stay here."

"My parents will worry," Echo objected.

"No, they won't," Billy said. "They'll just figure you're spending the night. Heck, you practically grew up over here. This is almost as much your home as it is ours. Remember when we used to go skinny-dipping in the creek?"

"At-loo-sha!" Echo and Mary Ann exclaimed together, glaring at the grinning Billy. Embarrassment gave Echo's skin an even deeper reddish hue than usual. She said, "That was a long time ago. We were children."

"Yeah, but I remember it."

"Young one, mind your tongue," Mary Ann snapped. "Daisy, help me with the stew. The rest of you, keep your places. We will bring the food."

The meal was a pleasant one. Fargo enjoyed the warmth of being surrounded by a family, something that was rare in his experience. And the food, a savory beef stew flavored with wild onions, was excellent.

When they had finished eating, Billy stood up and said, "I'm going to check on the animals one last time."

"I'll go with you," Fargo said as he got to his feet.

"Just in case there are any varmints around?"

"The thought crossed my mind," Fargo admitted.

For now, though, everything around the farm seemed to be peaceful. Fargo tended to the Ovaro while Billy made sure all the other horses and the cows had plenty of water and grain. They paused to lean on the corral fence, under thousands of stars that sparkled in the deep black night sky.

"Echo seems to be quite a woman," Fargo commented. "Beautiful and smart . . . and a mite feisty."

"She is, at that," Billy agreed with a chuckle.

"I'd say you're a lucky man."

Billy looked over at Fargo and sounded confused as he asked, "How come?"

"Well . . . you and her . . . I just figured that the two of you—"

Billy let out a laugh before Fargo could go any further with that line of thought. "You've got that all wrong, Skye," he said. "I love her, all right . . . like she was my own flesh and blood. I told you she was over here nearly all the time when we were growing up. Hell, she's almost as much of a sister to me as Daisy and Wa-nee-sha." The mention of the missing girl sobered him. "If I've still got two sisters, that is."

"We'll find Wa-nee-sha," Fargo vowed. "And we'll do everything in our power to bring her back safely to her family."

"I hope that's true . . . but after these past few

months, well, I'll believe it when I see it." Billy sighed. "Come on to the house. We might as well turn in."

Fargo jerked a thumb over his shoulder toward the barn. "I spotted a nice, comfortable-looking hayloft. Thought I might spread my bedroll up there."

Billy frowned in the starlight. "You'd rather sleep in a hayloft than in a real bed? Wouldn't you be more comfortable in the house?"

"Not necessarily. The life I lead, I might go for a long spell without ever sleeping in a bed, so I'm used to being without one. Anyway, if there's any more trouble tonight, whoever causes it might not be expecting me to be out here."

"Catch 'em in a cross fire, eh?" Billy rubbed his chin in thought. "Well, my ma won't like it. . . . She'll feel like we're not being hospitable enough . . . but what you say makes sense, Skye, just like always. I'll tell the folks what you're doing."

The two men said their good nights, and Fargo went back into the barn. He got his bedroll and his saddle and climbed the ladder to the hayloft. He had ridden a lot of miles that day, before getting involved in the trouble that had broken out several times since his arrival in this part of the territory, so he was tired and looking forward to stretching out for some rest.

He spread his blankets where the layer of hay was thin but still soft enough to serve as a mattress of sorts, positioned his saddle so that he could use it as a pillow, and then took off his hat and boots. He unbuckled the gun belt from around his hips, coiled it, and placed it on the floor of the hayloft next to his blankets where it would be handy if he needed it during the night.

Small scurrying sounds made him smile. The mice and rats who nested in the hay would keep him company tonight. He didn't mind. He felt a kinship with most animals, even the lowliest ones. As long as they didn't bother him, he wouldn't bother them.

Fargo crawled into his blankets, rested his head on the saddle, and closed his eyes. He thought he might ponder a little on the problems plaguing the Seminoles, but like a healthy animal himself, he was sound asleep in a matter of moments.

# 3

Fargo woke like an animal, too, going from slumber to full alertness in the blink of an eye. Hearing something that *wasn't* the scurrying of a mouse, he silently closed his hand around the walnut grips of his Colt and then, as boot leather scraped on the hayloft floor near him, he rolled over and brought the gun up. His thumb looped over the hammer, ready to pull it back and fire.

The figure looming over him in the darkness gasped and jerked back in surprise. "Mr. Fargo!" a familiar voice exclaimed.

"Miss McNally, what are you doing here?" Fargo asked coolly. He lowered the Colt.

"Why, I . . . I . . . It occurred to me . . ."

"What occurred to you?" Fargo asked when her voice trailed off and she didn't say anything else.

"I wanted to make sure you were comfortable—that's all." She paused. "Were you pointing a *gun* at me just now?"

Fargo grunted as he sat up and slid the revolver back into its holster. "You go sneaking around a man when he's sleeping, you've got to expect him to react a mite strongly when you wake him up."

"I'd hate to be the one who has to call you for breakfast in the morning, then."

Her acerbic tone brought a laugh from Fargo.

"Sorry," he said. "It's just habit. Sometimes people who wish me harm have tried to slip up on me in the darkness."

"But it's rather difficult to take you by surprise, I imagine."

"I've got pretty good instincts," Fargo admitted. He didn't add that if he didn't, he likely would have been dead a long time ago.

A glance through the little square door in the front of the hayloft told him that it was nowhere near morning. The night was dark as pitch. Echo wasn't carrying a candle or a lantern, so she must have known her way around the place pretty well in order to be able to find the ladder and climb into the hayloft without any light.

"Well, I'm sorry I disturbed you," she said as she turned toward the ladder. "I'll leave you alone now. . . ." She stopped, and he heard her take a deep breath. She turned back to him and said, "Actually, there's another reason I came out here."

"Oh?" Fargo said. "What's that?"

"To thank you. If those men had succeeded in carrying me off, Lord knows what would have happened to me. They might have done . . . anything."

Fargo shook his head, even though he knew she might not be able to see it in the darkness of the loft. "No thanks necessary," he told her. "I would have done the same for anybody."

"Yes, but it *wasn't* anybody you saved. It was me." He heard her moving closer to him, the hay crackling under her feet. "And I want to repay you."

He put a gruff edge in his voice as he said, "You already thanked me. That's plenty. You're welcome."

She reached out blindly. Her hand touched his chest. "Mr. Fargo . . . Skye . . ."

Fargo took hold of her wrist. "Listen, Echo," he

said, using her first name as she had used his. "I was prepared to steer clear of you when I thought that Billy might be courting you—"

"Billy?" she interrupted. "Courting me? Heavens, no! He's more like my brother than any sort of beau."

"Yeah," Fargo said, "he made that clear to me. Made me feel a mite better about finding you so attractive."

"You do?" She sounded a little surprised, and Fargo didn't think it was false modesty.

"I do," he said. "I think you're as pretty a woman as has crossed my trail in a long time. But that doesn't mean you're beholden to me in any way."

Her hand still rested on his chest, and his fingers still curled around her wrist. She leaned closer, and her other hand came up and stroked the short beard on his jaw.

"Then don't consider this my way of saying thanks or repaying any sort of debt to you," she whispered. "Just consider it something that I've wanted to do ever since I laid eyes on you."

She leaned closer still and kissed him.

Fargo brought his right hand up and cupped the back of her head as he returned the kiss, relishing the hot sweetness of her mouth. She was so close now that the tips of her breasts grazed his chest. He moved his other hand between them and stroked her right breast. His thumb found the hard nipple poking against the homespun fabric of her shirt and circled the sensitive nubbin.

Echo's lips parted eagerly as his tongue prodded against them. The warm, wet cavern of her mouth seemed to draw him in. Her tongue met his, dueled with it in a sensuous dance. Echo groaned low in her throat and pressed harder against Fargo. His hand tightened on her breast.

She pulled her head back abruptly, gasping for breath as her chest heaved. Fargo's hand shifted and found the beating of her heart, as he had earlier that evening when she'd fainted. Her heartbeat had been strong and steady then; it was even stronger now as arousal washed through her.

"You don't think I'm a wanton woman?" she asked in the heated darkness of the hayloft.

"I think you're a woman who knows what she wants," Fargo told her with a smile.

"And I want you, Skye Fargo," she said as she wrapped her arms around his neck and bore him over backward on the bedroll. She kissed him again.

They lay there wrapped up in each other's arms for a while, kissing and stroking and caressing until the excitement in each of them had grown too strong to be denied, even if they had wanted to. Echo sat up and tugged at Fargo's buckskin shirt while he unfastened the buttons on her garment, spreading it open so that he was able to fill both hands with her bountiful breasts. He cupped the firm globes and strummed the erect nipples. Echo tipped her head back and moaned in pleasure again before getting back to work on his clothes.

All tangled up with each other in the darkness like they were, getting their clothes off was a challenging task. They had to work at it by feel . . . which had definite rewards of its own.

Eventually they managed to strip each other naked. Echo wrapped both hands around Fargo's manhood, which by now jutted up like a long, thick iron rod from his groin. He felt her shifting around to bring herself closer to it, and then an exquisite sensation washed over him as her lips closed warmly around the head of his shaft.

As she sucked gently on him, he slid a hand down

her back, over the curves of her hips, and then between her legs, finding the fleshy folds of her sex. She
was already slick with desire, and he had no trouble
slipping a finger into her.

That made her suck harder on him. As he began to
work his finger in and out of her, she lifted her head
from his groin and gasped with pleasure. Fargo added
a second finger to his probing strokes and felt passion-
ate shudders ripple through Echo's body.

After a few moments, she whispered, "That feels so
good I don't want you to ever stop, Skye . . . but I
know something that will feel even better."

So did Fargo. He slid his fingers out of her and
grasped her hips, moving her around so that she strad-
dled him on her knees. She seemed to think that he was
ready to penetrate her, but Fargo wanted to postpone
that just a little while longer. He urged her forward so
that when he lifted his head, the musk rising from her
filled his nostrils and his beard brushed against the dark
triangle of wiry hair at the juncture of her thighs. He
extended his tongue and ran it along the heated furrow
of her femininity, pausing at the top to flick the most
sensitive spot of all before spearing it into her. .

Echo gave a low, throaty cry as she spasmed and
thrust her hips at him. Fargo continued licking, kissing,
and thrusting as Echo jerked and moaned, deep in the
grip of passion.

Finally, neither of them could stand to deny themselves the pleasure of the ultimate joining any longer,
and she slid back along his muscular torso until her
dripping sex was poised above his manhood. She
gripped the thick pole of male flesh, rubbed the head
between her nether lips until a slick mixture of their
juices coated it, and then slowly lowered herself onto
it until he was completely sheathed inside her.

She leaned forward and rested her hands on his

chest as her hips began to pump. Fargo matched her thrust for thrust. He cupped her breasts again and brought each of them to his mouth in turn so that he could suck the nipples. Echo rode him harder and faster. Fargo's heart slugged in his chest as he felt his own arousal growing to a fever pitch.

At that rate, it didn't take long for either of them to reach their culmination. Fargo shifted his hands from Echo's breasts to her hips and grasped them firmly as his hips arched upward from the blankets and his shaft drove to its deepest penetration yet. He froze there as he began to empty himself inside her. Echo shuddered in her own climax.

The shared moment seemed to last an eternity, but when it was finally over Fargo sagged back onto his bedroll and Echo slumped forward onto his broad, heaving chest. Fargo felt her heart pounding against him, and it seemed almost to be beating in time with his own. He stroked her back and her quivering flanks and pressed a kiss to the top of her head, inhaling the clean scent of her thick dark hair.

After a while she lifted herself slightly and gave a soft laugh. "What's funny?" Fargo asked.

Still a little breathless, she replied, "Now it seems that . . . I have something else to thank you for, Skye Fargo."

Fargo laughed, too, and tightened his arms around her. When he had thought that she and Billy were romantically involved, he had been prepared to honor that, as he had told her. He had even told himself that he didn't need the distraction of making love to Echo McNally.

But every man could use a little distraction every now and then, he told himself. Made the brain work better in the long run. . . .

Or so he hoped, anyway.

**41**

*    *    *

Echo had walked from the house to the barn by herself, but Fargo insisted on going back with her. He didn't think any troublemakers were still lurking around the farm right now, but you couldn't be sure about such things, especially with the way things had been going around here lately.

The night was as quiet and peaceful as could be, though, and after they parted at the back door of the house with a quick, soft kiss, Fargo returned to the barn, climbed up into the hayloft again, and within seconds of stretching out, fell into a deep, dreamless sleep.

He didn't wake up until just before dawn the next morning, when Billy called from down below, "Hey, Skye! Time to rise and shine, amigo!"

Fargo crawled out of his blankets, stood up, and stretched, working the kinks out of stiff muscles. He pulled his boots on, strapped the gun belt around his waist, and settled his hat on his head before climbing down the ladder.

Young Charley McCloud had come out to the barn with Billy. He sat on a stool milking one of the cows, the stream of milk hissing into a wooden bucket. He called, "Mornin', Mr. Fargo. You sleep all right?"

"Morning, Charley," Fargo replied, then thinking of Echo, he answered the young man's question. "I slept just fine, thanks."

Billy jerked a thumb over his shoulder toward the house. "Go on in and get some breakfast, Skye. Time you're done eatin', the sun will be up and we can take a better look around in those trees."

That sounded like a good plan to Fargo. He went in the house and found the place full of delicious aromas like coffee and pan bread and bacon. Echo sat at the table and smiled at Fargo as he came in. "Good morning, Mr. Fargo," she said primly.

Fargo tugged on the brim of his hat. "Ma'am," he greeted her just as formally. He figured Echo would appreciate the discretion on his part. She might not be ashamed of what they had done the night before, but she wouldn't want to flaunt it, either.

Cam-at-so came into the room and gave Fargo a dignified nod. "The night passed peacefully," he commented.

"That it did," Fargo agreed.

"But peace is a fleeting thing," Cam-at-so went on. "It never stays for long at a time."

"That's all too true," Fargo said. "Billy and I are going to do our best to see that it does, though."

Cam-at-so shook his head. "My son has never been one to seek out peace. That is why he rode with the white man's army, the same army that killed our people in Florida, in the old days. And even though he has returned, I can still see the restlessness in him. He was not made for the quiet, simple life of a farmer."

Fargo thought that was probably true about Billy. He had the same fiddle-footed nature as Fargo himself, and the day would probably come when he rode away from the farm again. When he did, he might not come back.

At the moment, though, with the crisis that gripped the area, Fargo knew that Billy wanted only to help his family and rescue his sister from whatever fate had befallen her. He could depend on Billy.

The breakfast Mary Ann set before him was every bit as good as the supper the night before had been. Billy and Charley came in while Fargo was eating, and Billy said to Echo, "Charley is going to ride back over to your folks' place with you, just in case."

"I'm not sure that's necessary," Echo replied with a frown.

"I am," Billy insisted. "Those varmints who've been snatching girls have never bothered any who had a man around." Billy grinned and punched Charley lightly on the arm. "Charley may not hardly qualify, but I reckon he'll do in a pinch."

"And I'd be mighty pleased to ride with you, Miss Echo," Charley said, a brick red flush creeping over his face. Fargo figured that Charley had a bit of an adolescent crush on Echo, and he couldn't blame the boy a bit for feeling that way.

She gave in and nodded. "All right. Thank you, Charley."

A short time later, Fargo and Billy saddled their horses and rode out to the trees where the attackers had hidden the night before. The sun had risen by now, and rays of reddish gold light slanted under the spreading branches of the trees. Fargo dismounted and walked slowly over the area, peering at the ground as he did so. From time to time, he paused and hunkered on his heels to study something even more closely.

Billy's expression grew more and more impatient as he waited. Finally he said, "Finding anything, Skye?"

"Their horses were shod," Fargo said. "In some places, that would mean they were white men. Not necessarily here, though."

"Yeah," Billy agreed. "Putting shoes on our horses is one of the things the Seminoles have picked up from the white men. Anything else?"

Fargo reached down and picked up something from the ground. He held out his hand and showed Billy the empty cartridge case that lay on his palm.

"They left some of their brass behind. They were firing Henry rifles, like mine. Those rifles are new enough, and expensive enough, so that we can say the gang is well armed. They've got money." Fargo scratched at his jaw as he frowned in thought. "And hombres who *have* money are usually pretty interested in acquiring *more.*"

Billy waved a hand. "This isn't really telling us anything."

"Sometimes little things add up to quite a bit," Fargo pointed out. "A few of those horses have distinctive nicks and scratches in their shoes. I'll know the hoofprints if I ever see them again."

Billy accepted that claim with a nod. Fargo had a phenomenal memory for such details.

"Let's ride up to the top of the rise where those two varmints tried to grab Echo," Fargo said as he reached for the Ovaro's dangling reins. "I want to take a look at any tracks they might have left."

As they circled the farmhouse and rode in the direction of the rise, Billy said, "They had already broken off the attack on the house when they jumped Echo. A couple of them must have spotted her and looped around like we're doing. We were in the house, so we wouldn't have seen them. They went after her because they wanted to get *something* out of the raid." He caught his breath suddenly. "Oh, hell, Skye. I just figured it out. They wanted Daisy, and they were ready to kill the rest of us to get her. Everybody's scared and keeping their womenfolk under guard now, so there aren't any gals out on their own for the gang to kidnap."

"Except for Echo," Fargo pointed out.

Billy rolled his eyes and said, "Yeah, except for gals like Echo who are too blasted stubborn and independent for their own good. Anyway, since those bastards can't get women one way, they've started attacking out in the open now and are willing to kill to get what they want."

Fargo nodded. "Could be," he allowed. "Let's take a look at the tracks they left."

Fargo found the spot where Echo's wagon had been parked and dismounted to scrutinize the ground around it. Billy joined him and pointed. "There are the hoofprints they left. They probably match up with some of the ones you saw over yonder in the woods."

"Hard to tell," Fargo murmured. "There's nothing too unusual about these."

"Maybe not, but when we find one of those sons o' bitches, I'll bet we find them all."

"Let's hope so," Fargo said with a nod. He swung back up into the saddle. "We'll see how far we can follow this trail."

When the two would-be kidnappers had fled the day before, they hadn't been trying to conceal their tracks. All they had cared about was getting out of there with their hides intact before Fargo ventilated them. Because of that their trail was easy to follow as it led west toward a low range of hills. The two riders had crossed several creeks along the way, but each time Fargo was able to pick up the trail again on the other side of the stream.

"I'm pretty good at reading signs," Billy said, "but I think they would've lost me by now, Skye. I'm sure glad you were able to ride down here and give us a hand."

"I haven't accomplished much yet," Fargo said.

They rode on, and after a while Billy commented, "I'm a mite surprised these hombres haven't joined up with the rest of the bunch yet. I figured they would have done that after they failed to grab Echo. Maybe they all make a habit of splitting up and heading back to their hideout by different routes, though."

"Some gangs will do that," Fargo agreed. "It's

harder to follow the trail of one or two men than it is that of a big bunch."

As if to confirm what he said, the tracks they were following disappeared a short time later while crossing a rocky stretch of ground. Fargo and Billy searched for the trail for another hour before admitting they had lost it.

"Damn!" Billy said as he pounded his right fist into his left palm. "I was hoping they'd lead us right to wherever they've been holding those girls they snatched."

"You knew it couldn't be that easy," Fargo said with a grim smile. "These hombres have had their own way around here for several months. They're not fools."

Billy gazed off toward the hills. "I'll bet they're up there somewhere. That's pretty rugged country. Plenty of places for folks to hide who don't want anybody finding them. We might search for a month and not come across them, Skye."

Fargo nodded. "That's why we have to come up with some other way to get at them. Let's head back to your folks' place."

It was past noon when the two men reached the farm. Billy's mother had kept food warm for them, though, so they were able to enjoy a late lunch and let their mounts rest for a while before they rode out again.

Charley was there and reported that Echo had reached her parents' farm without any trouble. "Didn't see anybody except a few folks who have farms between here and there," the youngster said. "Did you have any luck trailing those fellas who tried to carry her off?"

Billy shook his head. "We followed them toward those hills west of here but then lost their trail."

Charley stared at Fargo in surprise. "You lost a trail, Mr. Fargo?"

"Happens to the best of us, son," Fargo told him with a smile. "The trick is not to let that keep you from trying again. This afternoon we're going to follow those hombres who were hiding in the trees and taking potshots at you folks yesterday evening."

Charley's eyes widened with excitement. "Can I come along?"

Billy spoke before Fargo could reply to the boy's question. "I don't think that would be a good idea, Charley," he said. "Even if we do find the gang, we don't plan on taking on the whole bunch by ourselves. Still, it could be dangerous, and I'd rather you stayed here."

"Aw, Billy, I can take care of myself," the young man protested. "And I'm a good shot—you know I am."

Billy shook his head. "I know it, but you're staying here anyway."

Charley turned to Cam-at-so. "Don't you think it'd be all right for me to go along?" he insisted.

The older man said, "I agree with At-loo-sha. You should leave this task to him and Mr. Fargo. They know what they are doing."

Charley clearly didn't like it, but he gave up the argument. "You're gonna wind up tangling with those varmints, I just know you are," he muttered. "And I'm gonna miss the whole thing!"

A short time later, Fargo and Billy saddled up and rode out again, this time heading for the trees that had provided cover for the bushwhackers. Picking up the trail proved to be no problem, because at least a dozen men had ridden away from there in a hurry. The tracks stood out clearly on the ground.

The trail started out heading west, although not

along the same exact route as the one Fargo and Billy had followed that morning, but after a short distance it curved rather sharply south. Fargo reined in to look at it and frowned. "I never saw the tracks of those other two veering off from this bunch. That's a mite odd."

"Maybe we just missed their tracks," Billy suggested.

Fargo shook his head. "Nope, I was watching for them. It looks like the two who went after Echo weren't with this bunch after all, like we thought before."

"But they had to be," Billy said. "Maybe they didn't take part in the attack on the house, but they still have to be part of the same gang."

"Seems likely," Fargo said. "Come on, let's see where this group was going."

They followed the tracks south. Fargo knew that if they kept going in that direction, eventually they would come to the Canadian River. It was a small stream where it crossed the Texas panhandle, a long ways west of here, but this far downstream it was a good-sized river as it wound its way eastward to the point where it merged with the Arkansas River not far from Fort Smith. The river also formed the southern boundary of the Seminole lands in Indian Territory.

Around midafternoon, Fargo and Billy came out on a high bluff overlooking the river. The tracks they had been following turned east to follow the bluff. "Must be a trail down to a ford somewhere in that direction," Fargo mused. He and Billy turned their horses and began riding slowly along the bluff, their eyes on the tracks.

They hadn't gone very far when Billy suddenly reined in and said, "Damn it, my horse's gone lame." As Fargo brought the Ovaro to a stop, Billy dismounted and lifted his mount's right front leg. He took a clasp knife from his pocket, opened the blade with his teeth, and started digging at the hoof. After a moment he nodded grimly. "Yeah, he picked up a rock under his shoe. I guess we'd better head back."

"You go on back to the farm," Fargo told him. "I'm going to follow this trail a ways farther and try to find how they get down to the river, anyway."

Billy frowned. "Damn it, Skye, you can't go after those bushwhackin' bastards by yourself. You'd be outnumbered at least a dozen to one!"

"I don't plan to get in a gunfight with them," Fargo said. "I just want to find out where they went and maybe where they've been holing up. A group that size can't go gallivanting all over the countryside at night and then disappear during the day without a pretty good hideout."

Clearly, Billy didn't like the decision, but after a moment he shrugged and nodded acceptance of it. "Be mighty careful, though," he warned Fargo. "They've made it plain they don't mind killin'. After you came down here to help me and my family, I don't want you windin' up like those other two fellas who went looking for the missing girls."

"I'll keep my eyes open," Fargo promised.

He rode on eastward along the river while Billy turned back north, leading the lame horse to let it rest for a while before mounting up again. Within a few minutes, some trees screened Billy from Fargo's sight.

The Trailsman turned his attention to the tracks they had been following. He could see the river below to his right, broad and slow moving, and the bluff overlooking it was dotted with trees and brush.

The sandstone slope dropped off steeply, but Fargo knew it was only a matter of time before there would be a place where riders could get down to the river. The question was, would the gang he was following take that trail, cross the Canadian, and continue on south, or would they keep riding east toward Arkansas?

Like all the land between here and the Arkansas state line, the country up ahead had been set aside for the Indians. Fargo knew that if he kept going in this direction, he would wind up in the Creek Nation, and he was aware of the long-standing hostility between the Creeks and the Seminoles. The tribes had been allies once in their fight against the white men, but many in the much larger Creek Nation looked down on the Seminoles, probably because of their prolific intermarrying with other races. When the tribes were first removed here to Indian Territory, Fargo recalled, the Creeks and the Seminoles had shared a reservation, until the abuses heaped on the Seminoles by the Creeks had led the government to set up a separate Seminole Nation.

At least, that was the way the Seminoles told the story, Fargo thought with a faint smile. The Creeks probably had a completely different perspective on the matter, and the actual truth was probably somewhere in between. That was how such things usually turned out.

As for Fargo, he didn't care about tribal politics. He just wanted to find those missing girls and women and see that those responsible for kidnapping them were brought to justice. If the trail led into Creek territory, though, he would have to wonder whether members of the rival tribe might be responsible for all the trouble.

About a mile from the spot where he'd parted company with Billy, Fargo reached a place where the bluff had eroded and formed a trail down to the river, just as he expected. And also as he expected, the hoofprints he'd been following led down that gentler slope.

The sure-footed Ovaro went down the path with ease, and Fargo found himself riding along a grassy bank about forty feet wide. The sandstone cliff loomed above him, bulging out in an overhang. Flooding in years past had probably been responsible for that formation, he thought. Water flowing swiftly along the base of the bluff had eaten away at the relatively soft sandstone.

A few cottonwoods grew along the riverbank, and when some birds suddenly exploded out of the top of one of them about fifty yards ahead, Fargo tensed. He had just started to reach for his rifle to pull the weapon from its sheath when a shot roared. Fargo had instinctively swayed to the side as he reached for the Henry, and that move saved his life. A bullet whistled past his ear, so close he seemed to feel the hot breath of its passage.

He kicked his feet free of the stirrups and rolled out of the saddle, snagging the rifle as he fell. With an agile grace unusual in a man so big and muscular, he landed lightly on his feet and threw himself behind a large sandstone boulder that had split off from the bluff and rolled down to the riverbank sometime in the past. Another bullet hit the rock and threw dust and stone fragments into the air just as Fargo ducked behind the boulder.

He levered a round into the Henry's firing chamber and then waved his hat at the Ovaro, signaling the stallion to get back. The well-trained animal whirled around and galloped back along the bank, out of harm's way. He would return when Fargo whistled for him.

More shots rang out. Fargo heard the slugs pounding against the rock, but he was safe as long as he remained where he was.

But he was also pinned down, unable to fight back, and he didn't like that a bit. From the boulder to the base of the bluff was about twenty feet. Quite a bit of brush grew along there, and Fargo thought that if he could reach the concealment of the thick growth, he might be able to work his way along the bluff into a position where he could get a shot at whoever had ambushed him. Getting there might be trickier than it sounded, though, because there was no cover along the way.

The first thing he had to do was buy a second or two. He moved an eye past the edge of the boulder and spotted a figure behind that distant cottonwood. Powder smoke spurted from a gun muzzle as the man fired again. Instantly, Fargo thrust the Henry's barrel around the rock and fired three times as fast as he could work the repeater's lever.

Then he dashed the other way, toward the bluff, breaking out into the open and running for all he was worth as shots roared and bushwhacker lead screamed through the hot afternoon air around him.

# 4

Fargo reached the base of the bluff without any of the bullets hitting him. He dived headlong into the brush, once again shielded from the view of the man who was trying to kill him.

He couldn't stay where he was, though. The bushwhacker had seen where he went into the brush and was already concentrating his fire on the spot. Bullets rattled through the branches and clipped leaves that fluttered to the ground around Fargo as he bellied down and crawled along the bluff.

The shots fell silent. Fargo didn't know if the hombre was reloading or just trying to figure out where he was.

A second later a voice lifted in a shout, and another voice answered. Fargo heard hoofbeats and bit back a curse. Sounded like the bushwhacker was getting some reinforcements.

Fargo continued crawling along the base of the bluff. He glanced up and saw that openings pitted the bulging sandstone face, some of them large enough for a man to crawl into. He was tempted to try to reach one of them, on the chance that it might lead into a cave that would provide a way back to the top of the bluff.

He considered that possibility unlikely, though. Chances were, the openings went only a few feet deep into the bluff, and if he climbed into one he would be in an even worse fix than he was now. One way or another, he was going to have to fight his way out of this mess.

More than one rifle opened up on him. Fargo thought that three or four men were firing now. He had moved far enough so that they didn't know exactly where he was, but if they continued peppering this whole stretch of brush with lead, one of the bullets would find him sooner or later. He needed some better cover. . . .

A minute later, he found it as he came to a vertical fissure where the bluff's face had split as a result of some geological disturbance in the past. The crack in the sandstone was maybe four feet wide and angled in to a depth of about four feet as well. Fargo crawled into the opening and stood up, pressing his back against the rock.

He couldn't see the riflemen from here, which meant they couldn't see him, either. Nor were they likely to hit him with their shots unless they got lucky with a ricochet. He stood there for a long moment, catching his breath.

Then he tipped his head back and gazed up above him, his eyes following the fissure. He lifted his right foot and rested the sole of his boot against the opposite wall, pushing against it. A grim expression etched his face as he nodded. What he was considering was possible, but he didn't know where it would lead him since he couldn't see how far up the bluff the fissure ran.

It was a chance, though, which was more than he had charging four guns head-on.

Fargo pushed even harder against the rock, bracing himself tightly in the crack. He supported himself with his right foot and lifted his left, planting it a little higher. Then, holding the Henry at a slant across his chest, he wiggled his shoulders and worked his back a few inches up the fissure.

It was a good thing he wore tough buckskins, he thought. Otherwise even the relatively soft sandstone might soon shred his back to ribbons. One foot at a time, he shifted his position and maneuvered his way higher.

Along the riverbank, the guns still roared. The men hadn't given up on killing him. Since he wasn't shooting back, though, eventually they would hold their fire and start trying to decide if they wanted to risk going to check on him, to see if he was dead. By the time they did that, Fargo intended to be a good distance up the fissure, maybe even at the top of the bluff if it went that far.

Unfortunately, the riflemen's patience didn't last that long. The guns fell silent, and a man called out, "Bastard's gotta be dead by now, don't he?"

"You'd think so, as much lead as we poured in there," another rough-voiced man answered. "Sanders, go see if he's still alive."

"Me?" yet a third man yelped. "If he ain't dead, that's a good way for me to get shot, Rafferty."

"Maybe I'll shoot you if you don't do what I tell you, damn it!" the man called Rafferty responded.

"Why don't you make Chupco or Brunner go?"

"Ah, hell," a fourth man rumbled. "Let's all go. The son of a bitch can't get us all, and I'm willin' to take my chances."

Rafferty must have been thinking that over, because after a few seconds of silence he said, "All right. We'll do what Brunner said. Everybody spread out. First sign of movement or noise from that brush, we all open fire again. Got it?"

Mutters of understanding came from the other three

men. When Fargo listened closely, he could hear their cautious footsteps as they approached the brushy stretch along the base of the bluff.

This was as far as he could go, he realized. He had managed to wedge himself about a dozen feet up the fissure. Even though he hadn't been able to escape, he still had the element of surprise on his side. They wouldn't be expecting him to be above them.

Holding his breath and remaining absolutely motionless, the Trailsman waited. The four men were coming from behind him. They talked among themselves in low voices, speculating about who he was and whether they had killed him with their fusillade.

"I think he's the fella who rode down the hill at Buzzard's place," one of the men said, confirming that they belonged to the bunch that had attacked the farm. Fargo hadn't had any real doubts about that, but it was nice to know for sure that he had found his quarry.

"Must be one o' Buzzard's friends," Rafferty said. "I never saw him around here before."

"Be just like that son of a bitch to yell for help."

That comment brought a frown to Fargo's face. The men were talking like they knew Billy quite well, but the former scout had acted like he had no idea who they were. Something was really off-kilter here. . . .

But Fargo would have to stay alive in order to find out what it was.

He saw movement from the corner of his eye as one of the men stepped into his range of vision. A second man followed him an instant later, then the other two came into view as well. About fifteen feet separated each man as they warily approached the bluff. They were concentrating so hard on watching the brush where they believed Fargo to be that for several heartbeats none of them even glanced up.

That gave him time to swing the Henry into position to start the ball all over again.

He lined the muzzle on the man at the right end of the line, since that shot was at the easiest angle for him. The rifle's movement must have snagged the man's attention, because he finally looked up, his eyes widening and his mouth opening to yell as he saw Fargo perched in the fissure.

Before the man could make a sound, Fargo's finger squeezed the Henry's trigger. The rifle cracked and kicked against his shoulder, and the man went back a step as the bullet slammed into his chest.

Fargo dropped his legs as soon as he had fired, which sent him falling to the bottom of the crack in the bluff. He worked the Henry's lever as he fell. It wasn't a long drop, so even though the impact of his landing shivered from his soles up through his muscular calves and thighs, he didn't stagger or lose his feet.

The other three men reacted instinctively to Fargo shooting their companion. They jerked their rifles up and opened fire, spraying bullets into the fissure.

Luckily for Fargo, their aim was too high and all the slugs did was cause a shower of dust and grit around him as they smacked into the sandstone well above his head. In the meantime he brought the Henry to bear on another of the men and triggered a second shot. This one busted the hombre's shoulder and spun him around. Howling in pain, he pitched to the ground.

Fargo had cut the odds in half in little more than the blink of an eye . . . but unfortunately he was still outnumbered two to one. He threw himself to the side as the remaining two gunmen adjusted their aim and sent hot lead fanging at him.

Fargo landed behind the screening brush, rolled over, and stretched out on his belly as he fired upward at an angle through the branches. That was enough to scatter the two men who were still on their feet.

Eyes darting from side to side as he tried to locate his enemies, Fargo scrambled up. A shrill whistle came from his mouth. Almost instantly, hoofbeats pounded nearby. A gun roared, followed by the whine of a ricochet as the bullet missed Fargo and hit the stone wall behind him. He tracked the Henry toward the sound of the shot and fired, but he didn't know if he hit anything.

Then he spotted one of the gunmen to his right, drawing a bead on him. Fargo had a split second to realize that he wouldn't be able to bring his own rifle to bear in time to stop the man from firing.

He didn't need to, because at that instant the Ovaro loomed up behind the man, galloping toward Fargo. The man heard the thundering hooves and tried to get out of the way, but he wasn't fast enough to avoid the stallion entirely. Instead of trampling him under steel-shod hooves, the Ovaro clipped his shoulder as he raced past. The impact was still enough to send the man flying through the air. He crashed to the ground, rolled over a couple of times, and then lay motionless in a limp sprawl.

That left Fargo with only one enemy to deal with, but that man had gone to ground in the brush, too, and as Fargo came up in a crouch, he couldn't locate the lone remaining gunman. He turned slowly, holding the rifle steady as he scanned the thick growth.

The man burst out of the bushes with a yell. Fargo caught a glimpse of a blocky head and angry, twisted features in a red-hued face. Like the other three, the man was an Indian, although he wore white man's clothing. Those facts barely had time to register on Fargo's brain before the man crashed into him and knocked him over backward.

The impact as Fargo's back slammed into the ground jolted the rifle out of his hands. The man he was fighting no longer carried a rifle, and Fargo wondered fleetingly if he had run out of bullets for the weapon.

It didn't really matter, because at the moment the only important thing was that the man's hands locked around Fargo's throat and started trying to squeeze the life out of him.

The man had a knee planted painfully in Fargo's belly, too. Better there than the groin, Fargo supposed. The man had caught him without much air in his lungs, so he knew he had to break the hold quickly or pass out.

And if he passed out, he wasn't confident that he would ever regain consciousness.

He heaved himself up and hammered a fist into the side of the man's head. The man grunted in pain, but his grip didn't loosen. In fact, he squeezed tighter with his hands and his knee dug harder into Fargo's guts. The Trailsman hit him again, but the man raised his shoulders and drew his head down, almost like a turtle pulling back into its shell. His skull seemed to be made of cast iron, for all the good Fargo's punches were doing.

Knowing that he would run out of air within seconds, Fargo drew his right leg up as high as he could and strained to reach the handle of the Arkansas toothpick that rode in a fringed sheath strapped to his calf. His fingers brushed the leather-wrapped handle of the knife, but from this angle he couldn't quite get a good enough grip to pull it from the sheath.

The Indian must have figured out what Fargo was trying to do. He twisted his head to look and then started choking Fargo even harder. He pulled Fargo's head up off the ground and slammed it back down. Stars swam in front of Fargo's eyes. He lunged for the knife again, wrapped his fingers around it, and jerked it free.

The next second he had it planted in his enemy's side, shoving the long, heavy blade through flesh and feeling it rasp against bone as it scraped past the ribs. The man's eyes opened incredibly wide and his mouth gaped as he stared down at Fargo. Fargo drove the knife deeper, all the way to the heart.

The man tried to say something, but the only thing that came from his mouth was an agonized gasp. Then his face went slack, his fingers fell away from Fargo's throat, and he slumped forward. His deadweight pinned Fargo down for a second and still kept him from breathing, before Fargo got hold of his shoulders and shoved him aside.

Then Fargo was able to roll onto his side and lie there with his chest heaving as he dragged in great lungfuls of air. His throat hurt, and he knew it would be bruised. But that was a minor matter, especially as close to dying as he had just come.

After a moment, when his racing heartbeat had returned somewhat to normal, he pushed himself to his hands and knees and then to his feet. His iron constitution enabled him to shake off the effects of combat in a hurry.

The Ovaro suddenly whinnied a warning. Fargo whirled in the direction of the sound and saw a man leaping at him and swinging a rifle by the barrel, like a club. Fargo barely had time to recognize the man as the one who'd been knocked down and stunned when the stallion collided with him. Obviously the man had regained his senses.

Knowing that didn't do Fargo a damned bit of good.

The rifle stock crashed into the side of his head. He felt himself falling, but he was out cold by the time he hit the ground.

When he woke up, Fargo wasn't sure what hurt worse, his pounding skull or his bruised throat. One thing was certain, though—he was damned surprised that he had regained consciousness at all. If he'd had to guess, he would have said that the man who'd attacked him would have slit his throat while he was out cold.

But he was alive—nobody dead could hurt this bad—and as long as he drew breath he still had a chance to get out of this trap, wherever he was.

So, first things first. He kept his eyes closed so that his captors wouldn't know he was awake again, then began taking stock of where he was and what was going on around him.

He lay on his side on a hard, uneven surface, probably rock of some sort. His arms were pulled back painfully, and he couldn't feel his hands, so he figured that his wrists were tied together so tightly he had lost the feeling in them. He tensed the muscles of his legs just enough to confirm that they wouldn't move, meaning his ankles were lashed together, too. So he'd been tied hand and foot, trussed up like a hog going to market.

Fargo couldn't see anything, either. He moved his head slightly and felt something bind against his skin. A blindfold, he decided. His captors didn't want him moving around and didn't want him to know where he was.

He smelled wood smoke and heard the crackling of flames, but he didn't feel any heat coming from the fire, so he knew he wasn't lying close to it. In fact, the air around him had a dank chill to it. If he had been out in the sun, he would have been able to feel its warmth on his skin.

Yet he was conscious of a faint breeze brushing against his cheek. He was outside, not in a building, lying on rocky ground where the sun didn't shine.

A cave of some sort, thought Fargo.

And it was occupied, too. He knew that because of the fire. He didn't hear any voices, though, or anyone moving around. So maybe nobody was close to him, at least right at the moment.

He took advantage of the opportunity to bunch the muscles in his arms and shoulders and strain against his bonds. They were too tight. He didn't feel any give in them. Whoever had tied him up had known what they were doing.

He moved his head and felt the blindfold scrape against the ground. Maybe he could work it off or at least dislodge it enough to see a little. He had to know what obstacles he faced if he was going to get out of here.

He had barely gotten started, though, when he heard footsteps nearby, followed by voices that echoed slightly, another indication that they were in a cave.

"Think he's awake yet?"

"Hell if I know. Go back there and take a look if you want to."

"I'm still not sure why Rafferty wants him alive. He killed Chupco and Sanders, and Brunner won't be no good to us anymore with that busted shoulder. We ought to just cut the bastard's throat."

That was the sort of thinking Fargo expected from them. Rafferty, though, whoever he was, obviously thought differently.

The second man said, "I think Rafferty decided to keep him alive so he can take a long time dyin'. Rafferty wants him to pay for what he done. And he wants to know what this fella's connection is with Billy Buzzard, too. He said he was gonna ask him some questions as soon as he got back from lookin' for Billy."

There it was again, that familiar tone when one of them spoke of the former scout. That still made no sense to Fargo.

The first man said, "You know, I keep thinkin' that I've seen this man before. In Fort Smith, maybe. I feel like I ought to know who he is."

"He's a damned troublemaker—that's who he is. If he hadn't come along to lend a hand, we might've got Billy yesterday evenin'."

They hadn't said anything about the missing girls and women. Fargo had hoped that they might spill something useful on that subject.

"We'll get him," the other man said. "Thievin' bastard can't hide from us forever."

Now Fargo was genuinely confused. The next moment he became even more so, as the wind shifted slightly and brought the sharp tang of whiskey to his nose. Were the two men drinking? He hadn't heard them pull the cork from a bottle or say anything about taking a drink.

Hoofbeats rattled on rocks somewhere more distant than the two men who'd been talking, but not too far off. One of the men said, "Here come Rafferty and the rest of the boys. Maybe they found Billy."

The sounds of the horses grew louder and men's voices joined them. Several riders came up and dismounted. One of the first two men, who had been left there to guard him, Fargo had decided, called, "Any luck, Rafferty? Did you find him?"

"No," Rafferty's gravelly tones replied. Fargo sighed in relief, knowing that Billy had gotten away.

"We found some tracks. Buzzard was with this fella, all right, but they split up and Buzzard headed back toward his folks' place, the slick son of a bitch."

"If we was to burn 'em out, Rafferty, I bet they'd give the bastard to us," another man suggested.

"It's damn near come to that," Rafferty agreed, his voice ominous. "Wake that fella up. I want to talk to him."

Fargo started to stir, since his pose of unconsciousness had reached the end of its usefulness, but it didn't save him from having a bucket of cold water thrown in his face. He couldn't help but gasp at the shock of it.

Rough fingers dug under the blindfold and ripped it away from his eyes. He blinked at the sudden light as water dripped from his face. His sight adjusted quickly, and he saw that he wasn't in an actual cave, but rather a large, hollowed-out area underneath the overhanging bluff that ran along the northern bank of the Canadian River. He had no way of knowing how far this was from the spot where he'd had the fight with Rafferty and the other three men, but his sense was that it wasn't too far away.

The man who had knocked him out with the rifle hunkered on his heels in front of him. He had donned a flat-brimmed hat with a rounded crown, but it didn't improve his ugly, blocky looks any. He glared at Fargo and demanded, "You know where you are, mister?"

Fargo glanced past the questioner at the other men. He counted eight of them. They were Seminoles, some in traditional garb including feathered turbans, others dressed like white men. All were heavily armed and didn't look the least bit friendly.

"I'd say that I'm somewhere with a bunch of polecats," Fargo replied coolly.

Rafferty grunted. His right fist lashed out and caught

Fargo on the jaw, driving the Trailsman's head against the hard ground. "You just keep givin' those smart answers, mister," he said, " 'cause I can keep on givin' you what you just got all day if I need to."

Fargo tasted blood in his mouth. He ran his tongue over his teeth and didn't find any loose ones, so he figured that he was still in pretty good shape. He was about to tell Rafferty to go to hell when one of the other men exclaimed, "Now I remember him! I knew I'd seen him before, Rafferty. He's Skye Fargo!"

Rafferty turned his head to look at his excited subordinate. "Fargo?" he repeated. "The one they call the Trailsman?"

"Yeah. I saw him get in a shoot-out at the Ozark Palace Saloon over in Fort Smith a while back. Gunned down a couple of hombres just as slick as you please."

"I've heard about Fargo, too," another man put in. "He's supposed to be mighty dangerous. You better go ahead and kill him now, Rafferty."

"What's he gonna do?" Rafferty asked scornfully. "He's tied up so tight he can't move. Anyway, even if he wasn't, I ain't afraid of the high-an'-mighty Trailsman." He looked at Fargo again. "I am a mite curious what he's doin' ridin' with a low-down no-account like Billy Buzzard, though. How about it, Fargo? What's your connection with Billy?"

"He's my friend," Fargo said simply. He wasn't going to waste time or energy explaining to this man about how he and Billy had scouted together for the army, or how Billy had saved his life during that fight with the Pawnee war party.

Rafferty gave a harsh laugh. "Your friend, eh? Well, that comes as a surprise to me, Fargo. You know why?"

"I reckon you'll tell me," Fargo answered tightly.

"Damn right I will. I'm surprised because I never heard tell of Skye Fargo bein' friends with a no-good outlaw and whiskey runner like Billy Buzzard."

Fargo could only stare at him in incomprehension. Billy had a restless nature, but as far as Fargo knew he had always been on the right side of the law.

Rafferty chuckled. "Didn't know about that, did you? Billy used to be one of us. We load barrels o' whiskey on flatboats in Fort Smith and bring 'em up the Canadian River all the way to this cave. From here we sell the stuff all over Indian Territory. Biggest whiskey-runnin' operation in the territory, and it was all Billy's idea."

Fargo regarded the man grimly. Even though he was trying desperately to think of a reason why Rafferty would be lying about such a thing, he couldn't come up with one. Fargo was tied up and no threat at the moment, so Rafferty could afford to tell the truth.

Rafferty was shrewd and must have known what Fargo was thinking. "Don't want to believe me, do you?" he asked. "It's true, all right. Take a look over there."

He nodded toward Fargo's left, and when Fargo turned his head in that direction, he saw more than a dozen barrels lined up along the back of the cavelike overhang. The whiskey smell he had become aware of earlier came from them, he realized.

"Our stock's gettin' down kind of low," Rafferty went on, "but we got another boatload comin' in today. Ought to be here any time now. That's why we didn't want anybody comin' around, so I posted guards along the river both upstream and down. Then you rode along. Bad luck for you, Fargo." The man slipped a knife out of his boot and held the blade to Fargo's throat. "Now where's Billy got my money stashed? And don't tell me you don't know, because if you don't then I got no reason not to kill you."

Fargo had already deduced that there must have been a falling-out of some sort between Billy and the rest of the gang . . . assuming that Billy really had been part of the gang, and as far as Fargo could see, he had to accept that for now, no matter how much he disliked it. That the problem involved money came as no surprise. That was the only thing hardcases like Rafferty and the rest of this bunch really cared about.

Fargo felt the knife prick the skin of his throat. He could tell by the expression on Rafferty's face that the whiskey smuggler meant exactly what he said about killing him.

But Fargo couldn't tell Rafferty something that he didn't know. Billy certainly hadn't confided anything to him about any hidden loot.

Fargo got a reprieve, though, when a man called from outside, "Hey, Rafferty, the boat's here."

Rafferty glared at Fargo as he pulled the knife back. "I got to see about gettin' that whiskey unloaded. You just lie here and think about what I told you, mister. I'll be back."

Rafferty told a couple of the men to stay there and keep an eye on Fargo, then led the others outside the overhang. The riverbank here was a good fifty yards wide. The men had a wagon and a couple of mules that they took down to the edge of the stream. Fargo watched as other men poled a flatboat in to shore. Even from this distance and in his awkward position, Fargo could see that the boat was loaded with barrels like the ones already cached here.

Rafferty and his men got to work taking the barrels from the flatboat and loading them onto the wagon to be transferred up here under the overhanging bluff.

Fargo's mind worked furiously as he watched them going about their task. That load of whiskey represented a big profit for the gang. Liquor was forbidden here in Indian Territory, so naturally a thriving black market existed for it. If Rafferty and Billy really had been partners, they must have been making money hand over fist.

Those thoughts occupied only a small portion of Fargo's brain. He concentrated on figuring out a way to get free of his bonds and turn the tables on his captors. Unfortunately, he couldn't see any way of doing it. He was well and truly trapped.

And if Rafferty wanted to kill him, there wasn't a damned thing Fargo could do about it . . . except maybe spit in the outlaw's eye first and then die defiant.

Fargo wasn't the sort to give up, though. He could tell Rafferty some sort of lie about where Billy had hidden the money, and chances were that Rafferty would keep him alive until he'd checked out the story. Time meant life now, and Fargo would grasp all of it that he could.

The whiskey barrels were all stacked in the wagon, so many of them that the vehicle's bed sagged under the weight and the mules had to strain mightily against their harness in order to pull the load. Fargo watched as the wagon creaked up the slight slope to the overhanging bluff, followed by Rafferty and the rest of the gang. The wagon came to a stop just outside the cave-like area under the bluff. Now the barrels would be unloaded and rolled into place with the others.

Rafferty ordered the smugglers to get started on that chore, then walked back over to where Fargo lay. He stooped and pulled his knife from his boot again. "You ready to talk, Fargo?" he demanded.

"I'll tell you what you want to know," Fargo said.

Before he could say anything else, though, something odd happened. He saw what appeared to be a bundle of flaming rags drop down seemingly out of the sky and land right in the middle of those barrels of whiskey in the back of the wagon. The men who were unloading the barrels yelled in surprise and leaped to get away from there as fast as they could.

Then it seemed as if the whole world erupted in fiery chaos.

# 5

Two of the men who were trying to get away from the wagon didn't make it in time. They were still standing in the back of the vehicle when the explosion ripped out. Fargo saw them thrown into the air like rag dolls as flames engulfed their bodies.

Rafferty screeched curses as he ran a couple of steps toward the burning wagon. The heat forced him to stop as he lifted an arm to shield his face.

"Get that fire out!" he bellowed to his men. "Don't let it reach those other barrels!"

Flames licked hungrily toward the cache of whiskey under the bluff. When the makeshift bomb—because that was what it must have been, Fargo realized—had exploded in the back of the wagon, it had ignited the load of highly volatile liquor. The force of the blast had thrown burning whiskey for yards around, along with pieces of barrel and wagon that were on fire as well. If the swiftly spreading flames reached the other barrels against the rear wall, the resulting explosion might just bring down part of the bluff.

Still cursing, Rafferty swung toward Fargo and clawed at the gun on his hip. Fargo read the man's intent clearly on his face. Hundreds of dollars' worth of whiskey might be going up in smoke, but at least Rafferty would have the satisfaction of putting a bullet in the Trailsman.

Fargo was already moving as much as he could, though. He rolled onto his back and drew up his legs, then straightened them and kicked Rafferty in the knees.

Rafferty's legs went out from under him and the gun he had just yanked from its holster flew out of his hands. Fargo kicked again, this time catching Rafferty in the head. The outlaw stretched out on the rocky ground, knocked momentarily senseless.

That wasn't going to save Fargo's life, but at least he had the satisfaction of fighting back. Now he was going to try to get out of here, even though that was the longest of long shots. He rolled onto his belly and started crawling like a snake toward the exit, searching for a path through the spreading flames.

He hadn't gone very far when a figure suddenly appeared beside him and knelt, the flames glinting off the blade in the man's hands. Instead of plunging the knife into Fargo's body, though, he used it to sever the rawhide bonds around the Trailsman's wrists.

"Hang on, Skye!" Billy Buzzard said. "I'll get your feet loose!"

Billy cut those bonds, too, as Fargo pulled his numb arms and hands in front of him again. Pain shot through those extremities as blood resumed its normal flow through his veins. Billy sheathed the knife, got a hand under Fargo's right arm, and hauled him to his feet.

"Lean on me!" Billy told him. "We gotta get out of here!"

Fargo knew they didn't have much time left before the rest of the whiskey barrels went up. They moved awkwardly toward the open air, Fargo stumbling because his muscles didn't want to work right after being immobilized like that and Billy limping from his old injury. Flames leaped up on either side of them and heat beat at them like fists.

A man suddenly appeared in front of them, carrying a rifle. He tried to bring it to bear on them, but Billy whipped out a revolver and fired first. The bullet spun the whiskey smuggler out of their way. He dropped the rifle, which Fargo recognized as his own Henry. Billy grabbed it and handed it to him, and Fargo tucked it under his arm. They pressed on, and a moment later they emerged from the fiery, smoke-choked overhang and drew in lungfuls of cleaner, cooler air.

They weren't completely out of danger yet. The explosion had killed some of the gang and others were still trying to save the rest of the whiskey, but a couple ran toward Fargo and Billy, shouting curses and triggering guns.

Billy lifted his revolver and coolly blasted one of the men out of their way. Then he grunted in pain and stumbled, dropping the gun as he clapped his left hand to his right upper arm where a crimson stain suddenly appeared on his shirtsleeve.

Without hesitating, Fargo bent to scoop Billy's fallen Colt from the ground. The feeling hadn't completely returned to his hands yet, but he didn't have the luxury of waiting for that to happen. With Billy wounded, both their lives were now riding on his gun skill.

Fargo felt a tug on his buckskin shirt as he crouched and lifted the revolver. He knew a bullet had just come that close to hitting him. He thumbed off a shot of his own and saw the smuggler double over as the slug ripped into his midsection. The man's gun geysered flame again, but this time the bullet went harmlessly into the ground as he toppled over onto his face.

Fargo straightened from his crouch and asked Billy, "You all right?"

"Yeah, this is just a scratch," Billy replied as he nodded toward his wounded arm. "Let's go!"

They ran along the riverbank, leaving the overhang behind them. They hadn't gone very far when a roar filled the air and the earth suddenly jumped under their feet. Fargo glanced back over his shoulder and saw a fresh cloud of black smoke boiling out from under the bluff. Dust billowed out as well as a large section of the sandstone cliff sheared off and crashed down where the cavelike area had been, just as Fargo had thought it might if the rest of those barrels exploded.

"Reckon that's the end of Rafferty," Billy muttered. "Good riddance, too."

If Fargo had needed any further confirmation that Billy was mixed up with the whiskey runners, that was it, he thought grimly. But they could hash out all of that later. Right now, some of the outlaws might have survived that liquor-fueled holocaust back there, so it would be a good idea if he and Billy put some distance behind them.

He saw the means of doing so a moment later when he spotted the Ovaro and Billy's horse in a grove of cottonwoods. The reins of Billy's mount were tied to one of the saplings, but the Ovaro was loose and came trotting toward Fargo with a toss of his head.

"That big boy of yours wouldn't let me get his reins," Billy explained, "but he came right along with me, like he knew I was gonna try to get you loose from those bastards."

"How'd you manage to set off that explosion?" Fargo asked as they approached the horses.

"Tore some strips off my shirt to make a pouch and filled it with the powder I emptied from a dozen cartridges. Then I climbed up on that bluff over the cave and waited for them to park that wagon full of whiskey barrels right in front of it. That's the way Rafferty handled every shipment. I set the rags on fire and dropped the whole thing in the middle of the wagon bed. I knew it wouldn't take much of a charge to set off that whiskey."

"You know you could've blown me up, too," Fargo pointed out as the Ovaro nudged his shoulder. He patted the big black-and-white stallion's neck and then slid his rifle into the saddle boot.

Billy grinned. "Yeah. That's why I hustled down as fast as I could to find you. I didn't know what they'd been doin' to you, but I figured it couldn't be anything good, knowin' that bunch."

They paused there long enough for Fargo to take a look at Billy's wounded arm. As Billy had said, it wasn't much more than a scratch. The bullet had plowed a shallow furrow across the outside of his upper arm, creating a bloody but not serious wound. It took only moments for Billy to rip another strip off his shirt and for Fargo to tie it around his arm as a makeshift bandage.

"You'll need to get that cleaned up when we get back to the farm," Fargo told him.

"Yeah, I'm sure Ma will fuss plenty over it. It won't slow me down, though."

Billy jerked his reins loose and swung up into the saddle as Fargo climbed onto the Ovaro's back. He had a spare Colt in his saddlebags, so he wasn't worried about a handgun, but he was mighty glad he'd been able to recover the Henry.

"I thought your horse was lame," Fargo said as they started off. His fingers worked properly again now, so he got out that extra revolver and began loading it as he rode.

"He is, but he can carry me all right as long as I don't ask him to move too fast."

75

They rode along the river, heading back in the direction they had come from earlier in the day. Fargo didn't say anything until they had covered several hundred yards. When he spoke, it was without looking at Billy.

"I guess you must've heard the shots when that sentry first opened up on me."

"Yeah. I circled back and got there in time to see Rafferty taking you back to the hideout. He didn't see me, though. Not then, and not later when he came lookin' for me."

"You've always been pretty good about slipping away, haven't you, Billy?"

"Yeah," Billy replied, then looked over at Fargo and frowned. "What do you mean by that, Skye?"

"Your horse wasn't even lame, was it? You pretended to find a rock in its shoe and gouged its foot just enough with your knife to make it limp for a little while. Seems to be in pretty good shape now, though."

Billy's frown darkened until it was almost as black as the smoke still climbing into the sky behind the two men. "What the hell are you sayin', Skye? I don't think I like it."

"You didn't want to find that bunch," Fargo said, "but you couldn't think of any way out of going along with me when I started trailing them. You sure didn't want to cross paths with Rafferty again, though. Not after you double-crossed him and made off with his share of the profits from that whiskey-smuggling operation, as well as your own."

Billy gave a hollow laugh. "Is that what he told you? Hell, Skye, that's crazy! You know I'm not a whiskey runner."

"You know Rafferty, and you know an awful lot about what was going on back there." Fargo couldn't keep the accusatory tone out of his voice.

"In case you forgot," Billy said tightly, "I just saved your hide back there—again!"

"I know," Fargo said. "And I appreciate it. That's why I'm giving you the benefit of the doubt and waiting for you to explain what in blazes is going on around here."

"Damn it." Billy lifted a hand and wearily rubbed his face. "I didn't mean for things to get so mixed up. I really didn't."

"What's Rafferty got to do with those missing girls?"

Billy shook his head. "Not a blasted thing. When I wrote to you, Skye, it was because folks around here really needed your help. It didn't have anything to do with bringing whiskey into the territory. That's a business that Rafferty and I set up a while back. I didn't want you mixed up in it. I just wanted you to find out who's been kidnapping girls and young women from around here." Billy closed his eyes, put a hand to his temple, and shook his head. "Wa-nee-sha wasn't even missing then. I swear, Skye, if I had anything to do with that, do you think I would have put my own sister in danger?"

Fargo didn't say anything for a long moment, but finally he nodded and said, "I reckon I believe you about that part of it, Billy. Now tell me the rest of it."

"About the whiskey running, you mean?" Billy laughed, but the sound didn't have any humor in it. "What else was I gonna do, work on the farm? With this bum leg of mine, the army didn't want me as a scout anymore, and I can't carry my weight around the place. My pa and Charley have to do most of the work."

"I thought it was your decision to stop scouting for the army."

"Not really. I can't spend days in the saddle anymore. I wouldn't be any good on a long campaign. Just the riding we've done has been enough to get it to hurting pretty bad."

Fargo frowned. Billy had suffered that injury saving his life, and now it sounded like Billy was trying to make him feel guilty about it. Fargo appreciated what Billy had done, not only a couple of years earlier but also in getting him away from the gang of whiskey smugglers today. He would have risked his own life to save Billy's without a second thought, even now.

But he didn't like the idea of Billy trying to trade on that old debt or playing on his sympathies. Friends didn't do that.

"So you and Rafferty got together and decided to smuggle whiskey into the Nations," Fargo said.

"Yeah." For a second, Billy's usual cocksure grin returned. "Made a heap of money at it, too."

"Which you then turned around and stole from Rafferty."

"He doesn't have any proof I took it!"

Fargo took note of the fact that Billy wasn't denying the theft, just claiming that Rafferty couldn't prove he had done it.

"I decided I wanted out," Billy went on. "To tell you the truth, Skye, I saw what that whiskey was doing to some of the fellas we sold it to, and I didn't like it. My people have a hard enough row to hoe without being drunks."

"Noble of you," Fargo said coolly.

Billy flushed with anger. "Maybe you don't believe it, but it's true. I told Rafferty it was over, that we were gonna close everything down. He wouldn't go along with that. Threatened to kill me if I backed out of the deal."

"So you made him even fonder of you by stealing his share of the loot."

"I should've had a bigger share by rights!" Billy protested. "It was my idea to start with. I'm a mite ashamed of that now, but fair's fair. I didn't take all the money, just what I had comin' to me."

Fargo shook his head. Billy had changed in the time since Fargo had seen him last. Or maybe he hadn't. You could ride some hard, lonely trails with a man, even go into battle alongside him, without truly knowing him. Nobody ever really knew what was inside the other hombre's brain and heart and soul.

"I want to clear up a couple more things," he said. "Those night riders I've heard about . . . that was Rafferty's bunch?"

Billy nodded. "Yeah. They always made their whiskey deliveries at night."

"But they're not the ones stealing the girls, even though everybody around here thinks they're to blame?"

"That's right."

"And earlier this afternoon, you lamed your own horse because you didn't want to be with me when I ran into Rafferty and the rest of the gang."

"You're determined to make me admit that, aren't you?" Billy sighed. "All right. Yeah, I did it. I couldn't think of what else to do. I'm ashamed of it now, but I was scared. After Rafferty attacked the farm yesterday, I knew he wouldn't stop at anything to get what he wanted."

"They were just trying to throw a scare into you, right? So that maybe you'd give back the money you stole?"

Billy didn't even bother trying to rationalize it this time. "That's the way I figure it," he said. "They could've killed me and Charley while we were outside if they really wanted to. That was just Rafferty's way of tellin' me that he meant business." Billy looked back. The Canadian River was several miles behind them by now, and the smoke was no longer visible. The fire had probably burned itself out as soon as the flames consumed all the whiskey. "Well, he's *out* of business now, I reckon. We can forget about him and concentrate on finding those missing girls, including my sister."

"Maybe that's the way you hoped it would turn out," Fargo mused. "Half that bluff fell on Rafferty, so you don't have to worry about him anymore."

"Are you sayin' I sent you after him to get rid of him and take care of my problem for me?"

Fargo shrugged. "Somebody might think that."

Billy reined in sharply and said, "Damn it, Skye, I came back to help you. I could've just kept goin'. And you were tied up when I dropped that bundle of powder in the wagon. *I* saved *you*."

"There's no denying it worked out that way," Fargo admitted. "You saved my bacon, Billy. I'm obliged to you for that."

"Help me find Wa-nee-sha and those other girls, and we'll call it square."

"I always intended to help you find your sister," Fargo said. "Nothing that's happened today has changed that."

They rode on as an uncomfortable silence descended between them. Now that Fargo had found out more about Billy, he didn't much like being in his debt. He was, though, and there was nothing he could do about it except try to square things.

After a while, Fargo said, "Everybody I saw in Rafferty's bunch was Seminole."

"Yeah. After the way the government's treated us, especially lettin' the Creeks lord it over us like they did, you won't find many people around here who are worried too much about breakin' the law. What about it?"

"That hombre who took a shot at me yesterday when I first met Charley had red hair and freckles. He didn't look like any Indian I ever saw."

Billy shook his head. "I don't know who he was, but I can tell you that he wasn't one of Rafferty's bunch. We didn't have any white men working with us except the ones who supplied the whiskey in Fort Smith, and none of them had red hair. I'm sure of that."

"Then who was he?"

"One of the bunch that's been kidnapping those girls?" Billy suggested. "He could have even been one of the men who tried to grab Echo yesterday evening. You didn't get a good look at them, did you?"

Fargo shook his head. "Nope. She didn't say anything about either of them being redheaded . . . but I didn't ask her, either. So it's possible. I'll find out for sure the next time I talk to her." Fargo thought about riding over to her parents' farm. "Maybe tonight."

He hadn't forgotten how pleasant the time he'd spent in the hayloft with Echo had been.

Now that they were no longer following the trail of the men who had attacked the farm of Cam-at-so and Mary Ann, Billy led them back to the farm by a shorter route. Still, it was late in the afternoon before they neared the place. They had been in the saddle a lot today.

When Fargo glanced over at Billy, he saw that the former scout's face was drawn and lined with pain. That bad hip of his really did make it difficult for him to ride for a long time, Fargo decided.

"I'm going to explore those hills to the west some more tomorrow," he said, "but there's no need for you to come along. Might do you some good to rest a little instead.''

Billy's jaw took on a stubborn set as he shook his head. "Nothing doing, Skye," he said. "I'm comin' with you. You might need a hand, and I can still fight.''

"You're pretty good at thinking on your feet, too," Fargo said. "Tossing that bomb you made into the wagon was a pretty good trick.''

Billy smiled. "Yeah, it was, wasn't it? Even if I do say so myself.''

"But after all the riding you've done today—''

"Forget it, Skye. I'm going with you tomorrow, and that's final.''

Fargo didn't waste any more breath arguing. In the end, it had to be Billy's decision.

But if Billy couldn't keep up, Fargo would leave him behind. *That* would be Fargo's decision.

They came in sight of the smoke rising from the farmhouse's chimney. Fargo said quietly, "Before we get there, Billy . . . does your family know anything about your involvement with Rafferty?''

Billy shook his head. "Not a thing. I'll bet my pa wondered where I got my money sometimes—he's a pretty canny old bird—but he never said anything.'' He suddenly looked concerned. "You're not gonna tell them, are you, Skye?''

"You don't think they deserve to know who was shooting at them yesterday evening, and why?''

"Yeah, maybe they do," Billy admitted grudgingly.

"You ought to be the one to tell them, though.'' Fargo took a deep breath as he reached a decision. "I won't say anything to them.''

"Thanks, Skye. Now *I'm* obliged to *you*.''

That wasn't enough to even things up between them, though, and Fargo knew it.

He suspected that Billy did, too.

A short time later, they reached the farm. As they rode toward the small cluster of buildings, someone ran out of the farmhouse. Fargo recognized Charley McCloud's slender figure. The youngster ran toward them, and Fargo immediately sensed that Charley wasn't just glad to see them.

"Something's wrong," he said.

Billy recognized it, too. "Charley's upset," he said. He spurred forward. Fargo heeled the Ovaro into a run and quickly caught up with him.

Charley was panting and out of breath when they reached him and reined their mounts to a halt. Both men swung down from their saddles as Charley bent over, rested his hands on his knees, and gulped down air. When he looked up at them, his face was tight and drawn with fear.

"She's g-gone," he managed to say. "The kidnappers got her!"

Billy grabbed his arm and cried, "Who? Daisy?"

Charley shook his head. "No. Echo! They got Echo, Billy!"

# 6

Fargo stiffened in shock. He said to Charley, "I thought you took her back to her folks' place this morning."

The youngster nodded. "I did. But she started back over here this afternoon, Mr. Fargo. That's what her pa said. He got worried about her and rode over to make sure she got here all right, but we hadn't seen hide nor hair of her! We backtracked and . . . and found her wagon. Somebody had rolled it off the trail and hid it in some brush. They'd cut the mules loose and let 'em wander off."

"Get your horse and show me where you found the wagon," Fargo snapped.

"Wait a minute, Skye," Billy said. "The sun's almost down. You can't track in the dark. Not even the Trailsman can do that."

"If there's a bright enough moon . . ." Fargo began. He stopped when he realized that the moon was at its thinnest stage right now. Billy was right. Not even he could read sign by starlight.

"Why'd she have to come back here?" Billy asked with agonized worry in his voice. "What was so important she had to risk it, and why the hell did her pa let her travel by herself?"

Charley shook his head. "I don't know why she

came, Billy. And she didn't tell her pa she was headed over here. He was working in the fields when she left. You know how she is."

"Yeah. Too damned headstrong for her own good." Billy looked at Fargo. "What are we gonna do, Skye?"

Fargo's mind was a mass of anger and worry. He thought he might have an idea why Echo had decided to return to the farm. She could have wanted to see *him* again. Could have wanted to repeat the lovemaking they had shared the night before. And that desire could have led her into deadly danger.

He forced himself to think coolly and rationally. Stampeding off out of control wouldn't do anybody any good. "We were going to ride over to those hills west of here tomorrow anyway," he said. "Now we've got an even better reason to do that. If we can pick up the trail of the men who took Echo, I'm betting that's the direction it'll lead."

Billy nodded. "Yeah, I think so, too. Is Echo's father still here?"

Charley shook his head. "No, he went back home. He wanted to follow the trail himself, but Cam-at-so persuaded him to wait for you and Mr. Fargo, since he's an old man. He wouldn't stand a chance by himself against those varmints, even if he was able to find them." The boy's eyes widened as he noticed the bloody bandage tied around Billy's arm. "What happened? Are you hurt bad, Billy?"

"This?" Billy looked at his arm. "It's nothing. We ran into some fellas who took some potshots at us, that's all."

"Maybe they were the kidnappers?"

Billy shook his head. "No, they weren't. I'm sure of that. Just a bunch of no-account owlhoots—that's all."

Charley frowned, clearly puzzled about how Billy

could be so sure of that, but he didn't press the issue. He just said, "Your ma's gonna be upset that you're hurt."

Billy managed to grin. "If Ma didn't have anything to fuss about, she wouldn't know what to do with herself."

They walked on to the house, leading their horses. When they got there, Charley offered to take care of Billy's mount for him.

"I'd tend to that stallion of yours, too, Mr. Fargo," the youngster said, "but to tell you the truth, he scares me a little."

"That's all right, Charley," Fargo assured him. "I'll take care of him. Billy, go on in and have your mother take a look at that arm. The wound needs to be cleaned out good, so it won't fester."

"Never knew you to be such a mother hen, Skye."

"I owe you," Fargo said bluntly. "I want to keep you around long enough so that I can square things with you."

He left unspoken the idea that Billy should tell his folks about what he'd been doing since he came back to Indian Territory. Even though Billy had seemed somewhat receptive to doing so, Fargo didn't really expect him to go through with it. But one way or the other, that was up to Billy.

Fargo was a lot more worried right now about the fate of Echo McNally.

He and Charley unsaddled and rubbed down the horses, then made sure the animals had plenty of water and grain. By the time they went into the house, Mary Ann had Billy sitting in front of the fireplace with his shirt off as she cleaned the wound on his arm with warm water and a piece of cloth. As Billy had predicted, she was fussing both over and at him, worrying over the state of his wound and telling him that he shouldn't get into situations where people were shooting at him.

Billy wore a grin on his face, but his eyes were uneasy as he glanced at Fargo, who could tell that he hadn't said anything to his parents about the whiskey-running scheme. Fargo just shook his head. What Billy said or didn't say to his folks was his own business from here on out. Fargo washed his hands of the matter.

Cam-at-so came over to Fargo and said, "The boy told you of Echo's disappearance?"

"That's right," Fargo replied with a nod. "First thing in the morning, we'll pick up the trail of whoever grabbed her."

"My old friend Joseph McNally will join you. I tried to convince him to leave this to you and my son, but he would not listen." Cam-at-so shrugged. "With his daughter missing and surely in danger, I didn't really expect him to. I helped my son search for Wa-nee-sha at first, too, and my heart is still torn with worry."

Fargo wasn't too fond of the idea of being saddled with the old-timer, but he understood what Echo's father was going through. "If he can't keep up, we won't be able to wait for him," he warned.

Cam-at-so nodded. "I told him as much. He says that he will keep up and help find Echo, or he will die."

That was what Fargo was worried about. Like it or not, he would feel that he had to look after McNally as well as follow the trail of whoever had kidnapped Echo.

He took a look at the wound on Billy's arm before Mary Ann wrapped clean bandages around it and tied them in place. The furrow that the bullet had left behind hadn't done any serious damage, even though Billy's arm had to be pretty stiff and sore. Give it a week or two and he would be as good as new.

"Can you fire a gun with that hand?" Fargo asked.

"Hide and watch if you don't think I can," Billy replied with his usual cocksure grin. He must have decided that Fargo wasn't going to give away his secret, because he was his old self again.

Not as carefree as he had once been, though, because now his childhood friend Echo was missing along with his sister Wa-nee-sha and a dozen other girls and young women from the area. Fargo could tell from the look in Billy's eyes that the disappearances haunted him, too.

Fargo's instincts told him that whatever had happened to the missing girls, it couldn't be good. His gut said that they were running out of time, too, if they wanted to do anything to help those victims. If they didn't find out what was going on soon, chances were they never would. In fact, it might already be too late. . . .

But Fargo wasn't going to think that, because it would mean giving up.

And that just wasn't something the Trailsman was going to do.

He slept in the barn again that night, although the memories that the hayloft held for him were bittersweet ones now, with Echo missing and maybe dead . . . and maybe worse. But his reasoning in choosing to sleep in the hayloft the night before—so that he could surprise anyone who attacked the farm— were still as valid as they'd ever been.

Fargo's restless slumber left him stiff and gritty-eyed the next morning. His throat was bruised and his voice hoarse from the choking he had received the day before. A couple of cups of Mary Ann's strong coffee and a hearty breakfast helped with all those ailments.

"How's your arm?" he asked Billy.

"Fine." Billy moved the bandaged arm to demonstrate just how good it was, but the wince that appeared briefly on his face told Fargo that Billy still felt some aches and pains, too. "How about you?"

"I'll live," Fargo said curtly. He was anxious to ride out and try to pick up the trail of Echo's kidnappers, but he knew they would have to wait until the sky was light enough for them to see.

Charley came in from outside, where he had been tending to the early-morning chores with Cam-at-so. "Mr. McNally's comin'," he said. "He's armed for bear, too."

Carrying their coffee cups, Fargo and Billy went outside to greet Echo's father, who obviously hadn't changed his mind about accompanying them.

Dressed in traditional Seminole garb, including the buckskin leggings, long, loose-sleeved shirt, sash, and feathered turban, Joseph McNally looked like he was ready to go to war. Two cap-and-ball pistols were tucked into his sash, along with a knife with a long, heavy blade, and he carried a Sharps carbine. Twin bandoliers containing bullets for the Sharps crisscrossed his chest. When he dismounted, Fargo saw that he was taller and leaner than most Seminole men. He had long gray hair braided behind his head and startling green eyes that looked out from a rough-hewn face. He looked tough as knotty pine, and Fargo liked him instantly.

He was still a little worried about having to keep an eye on the man, though, so he was a mite reserved as he nodded and shook hands with McNally when Cam-at-so introduced them.

"I have heard much that is good about you, Mr. Fargo," McNally said. "I believe that with help from you and At-loo-sha, we will find my daughter."

"Darn right we're gonna find Echo," Billy said. He

drank the last of his coffee from the cup and handed it to Daisy, who had followed them out of the house along with Charley. "Let's get our horses saddled up, and we'll be ready to go."

"I will speak with my old friend Cam-at-so," McNally said with a grave nod.

Fargo drank the rest of his coffee and gave the cup to Daisy, too. Then he headed for the barn with Billy. Charley followed along behind them, carrying a lantern to dispel the predawn gloom.

Once they were in the barn, Charley asked in a low voice, "How about letting me come along, too, Billy?"

With a frown, Billy shook his head. "I don't reckon that'd be a good idea. We're liable to run into some pretty bad men. It'd take that kind to steal a bunch of girls and young women like that."

"But I can fight," Charley insisted. "I'm a good shot. I did fine during that ruckus a couple of days ago, when those men attacked the farm."

Fargo knew that they were after a different gang now, but Charley didn't. Fargo didn't say anything, just went about the business of getting the Ovaro saddled up and ready to ride.

"I know I shouldn't have run away when that fella bushwhacked Mr. Fargo," Charley went on. "I'd like to make up for that now."

Fargo said, "There's nothing to make up for as far as I'm concerned, Charley. You didn't know me, and you didn't know what was going on. You did the smart thing by lighting a shuck when you did."

"Well, I don't feel so smart," Charley said, "and I don't feel good about it, Mr. Fargo." He turned back to Billy. "How about it, Billy? Let me come with you?"

Billy shook his head. "Forget it. You're like a little brother to me, Charley. I got to look out for you and do what's best for you, and it's best that you let me and Skye handle this."

"You're letting Mr. McNally go along," the youngster protested.

"That's different. Echo's his daughter."

"Yeah, well, she's almost like a sister to you, ain't she?"

Billy shrugged in acknowledgment of that fact.

"And you just said that I'm like a little brother to you," Charley went on. "That would make me and Echo like brother and sister, too, wouldn't it?"

Billy laughed. "I swear, you'd argue with a coon and tell it that it wasn't sittin' in a tree, when all the time it was chunkin' acorns at your head." He clapped a hand on Charley's shoulder. "But you still can't go, and that's final."

Charley's face fell. He muttered something, turned, and went out of the barn, leaving Fargo and Billy to finish getting their mounts ready.

Billy glanced at Fargo. "I did the right thing by turnin' him down, didn't I, Skye?"

"Yeah, I'd say you did the right thing, Billy . . . this time."

Billy's face flushed in the lantern light. "I was gonna tell 'em about Rafferty and, well, about that whole ugly business, but everybody was so worried about Echo . . . I just didn't think it was a good idea to give them something else to be upset about right now."

Fargo had to admit that that reasoning actually made sense, despite being a little self-serving on Billy's part. "Finding Echo and those other girls is what's important," he said.

"You bet it is. Ready?"

Fargo nodded. "Let's get Mr. McNally and hit the trail."

McNally was ready to ride. He shook hands with Cam-at-so and swung up into the saddle with a litheness that belied his age. The three men heeled their horses into motion and set off eastward from the farm, heading toward the spot where Echo had been waylaid and carried off the day before.

The sun had not yet risen when they started off, but the sky had lightened enough for them to see where they were going. By the time they reached the place where Echo's wagon had been found, the brilliant orange ball had climbed halfway above the horizon, spreading its garish glow over the landscape.

McNally indicated a large clump of brush that grew to one side of the trail. "Behind those bushes," he told Fargo and Billy. They circled the thick growth and saw the wagon, which still sat right where it had the previous day when McNally, Cam-at-so, and Charley had discovered it.

The mules were nowhere in sight, and the harness that had attached them to the wagon had been cut. Fargo confirmed that by checking the ends of the harness that remained. He dismounted and walked slowly around the vehicle. He saw no signs of blood on the wagon seat or anywhere else around it, and he was grateful for that.

The tracks of four shod horses mingled with those of the mules. They came up on both sides of the wagon, as if the riders had surrounded Echo and forced her to drive back here in the concealment of the brush. It would have been simple then to pluck her off the seat, throw her over the saddle of one of the riders, and gallop off with her, leaving a man or two behind to cut the mules loose and haze them out of the vicinity so they wouldn't draw attention to the empty wagon.

"Did you find her shotgun?" Fargo asked McNally.

The old man shook his head. "No, the kidnappers must have taken it with them, too."

"Wonder if she got a shot off," Fargo mused.

Billy said, "She would have unless they took her completely by surprise. Echo isn't the sort to give up easy."

"At-loo-sha speaks the truth," McNally agreed. "My daughter would fight if she could."

Fargo had seen the evidence of that with his own eyes, a couple of days earlier. He knelt and studied the hoofprints left behind by the kidnappers' horses. "Nothing unusual about these tracks," he announced as he straightened and reached for the Ovaro's reins. "Let's see if we can follow them."

The trail meandered a little, as if the kidnappers had been trying to throw off any pursuit, but Fargo was able to follow it as it led generally westward, skirting well north of the farm where Billy lived and heading toward that low range of hills in the distance.

"Either of you know much about those hills?" Fargo asked.

McNally shook his head. "I have never been there. I have always stayed close to my own farm."

"I rode over there a few times when I was a youngster," Billy said. "You know, just exploring like a kid will do. They're pretty rocky, and honeycombed with caves. Go on past them, and the ground sort of drops away into some mountains."

Fargo glanced over at him with a frown. "Drops into mountains instead of rises into them?"

"Yeah. You'll be ridin' along on what seems like relatively flat land, and then all of a sudden you're on top of a mountain with big canyons on either side of you. Sort of like those canyons over in the Texas panhandle, only there are a lot more trees around here."

Fargo had been through the Palo Duro country, a highly dangerous part of the panhandle that was home to numerous bands of warlike Comanches, so he understood now the sort of terrain Billy was talking about.

"Sounds like that would make a pretty good hiding place for anybody who didn't want to be found," he commented.

"Yeah, the same thought was starting to cross my mind," Billy said with a nod. "It's a good day's ride over there. Maybe we should've brought more supplies than we did."

McNally slapped a canvas bag tied to his saddle. "I have provisions enough for several days," he told them. "I left home knowing that I would not return without my daughter."

Fargo smiled. "We ought to be all right, then. And it's not like we can't rig a few snares if we need to."

They rode on, continuing to follow the trail as it trended westward toward the hills. The more Fargo thought it, the more he believed that their destination lay not in the hills themselves but in the more rugged country beyond them that Billy had described. The gang of kidnappers would find even more good places to hide there.

The kidnappers had ridden across rocky stretches of ground and along streambeds, but every time it began to seem that the trail had disappeared, Fargo found it again. McNally looked on in amazement as Fargo's eyes saw what few men could even begin to discern.

"I am told that you are called the Trailsman," the old Seminole said. "Now I understand why. I would have believed that no white man could read sign as well as an Indian . . . and I would have been wrong."

"I've been blessed with good eyesight and good instincts," Fargo said. "It's nothing I can take credit for. Any bragging rights belong to the Good Lord."

"Blessed is right," McNally said. "And I hope our efforts to find Echo and Wa-nee-sha and the other missing girls are blessed as well."

Fargo nodded in agreement with that sentiment.

He called a halt around midday, and the three men let their horses rest while they made a simple meal of jerky and biscuits, washed down with water from their canteens. The stop was only a short one, and soon they were back in the saddle.

Fargo glanced back a couple of times during the afternoon, and the second time Billy noticed. "Something wrong, Skye?" he asked.

"Just checking our back trail," Fargo replied. "I wouldn't swear to it, but I've got a funny feeling that somebody's following us."

Billy hipped around in his saddle and gazed behind them. "I don't see anything," he said after a moment.

"I didn't, either. But I'm still not convinced that somebody's not on our trail."

Billy nodded. "I trust your instincts. We'll keep a close eye out."

"I think that'd be a good idea," Fargo said. "It's possible the gang left somebody watching that wagon, so that they could follow along behind any pursuers and maybe ambush them."

Despite his increased vigilance, Fargo didn't spot anyone following them as the afternoon wore on. The trail became easier to follow, as if the kidnappers had been convinced by the time they came along here that no one could be tracking them anymore.

By late afternoon the three men were in the hills. At the edge of the slopes they had found the remains of a campfire where the kidnappers had stopped the night before. Fargo had taken a close look around but found nothing to indicate exactly what had happened here.

All they could do was hope for the best.

The trail wound around more now as the riders followed the easiest route through the rugged terrain. Thick woods covered the slopes, and brush choked most of the gullies between the hills. A fella would have to know where he was going in order to get through here without a lot of trouble and slow going. The kidnappers were obviously familiar with the best route, and by following their trail, Fargo, Billy, and McNally were able to reach the far side of the range by the time the sun began to slide below the western horizon.

It had been a long day already, but Billy and McNally didn't want to stop. "This strip of prairie in front of us isn't very wide," Billy explained. "It's just a couple of miles to where those mountains or canyons or whatever you want to call 'em start. I think we ought to ride on that far before we make camp, anyway."

"I agree," McNally said. "I feel that we are close to those we seek."

"All right," Fargo agreed. "But it'll have to be a cold camp tonight. We don't want to tip them off that we're this close."

That was fine with the other two men. Fargo pointed out where the hooves of their quarry's mounts had flattened some of the grass, and they were off on the hunt again.

Billy was right about it not being far to the more rugged terrain they sought. The trail led straight across the plains that were dotted here and there with trees. Then, just as Billy had described, the ground suddenly dropped away in a steep slope in front of them. Fargo,

Billy, and McNally reined to a halt and peered out across miles of brushy, wooded, rocky wilderness. The ridges and canyons that formed this mountain range twisted and turned in a serpentine maze.

"There are caves here, too," Billy said. "I found a couple, and there are bound to be more because I never went very far in there. To tell you the truth, I was a mite scared. To a kid it looked like the sort of place where varmints might be lurking."

"You were right about that," Fargo said. "I'd stake my hide there are varmints hiding somewhere out there right now . . . the varmints we're looking for."

"Should we go ahead?" McNally asked.

Fargo shook his head. "There's not enough light left." Already the waning sunlight left the canyons cloaked in deep shadows. "We'd be better off getting a fresh start in the morning."

Billy and McNally went along with that, although both men were clearly tense and anxious to continue the search for the missing women and girls.

They found a good spot to camp, a clearing in the brush that would give them some concealment in case of trouble. Billy and McNally hobbled their horses after they had unsaddled them, but Fargo left the Ovaro free. The stallion's keen senses and combative nature made him an excellent sentry, and he never strayed far from Fargo's side.

Supper was jerky and biscuits and canteen water again, as well as some apples that McNally had brought along. The men ate as darkness gathered around them. Yawns were common. They had ridden a long way today and were tired.

They had just begun to discuss the order in which they would stand guard during the night when Fargo noticed the Ovaro's ears pricking up. The stallion stopped cropping at the grass and lifted his head, peering off to the east, toward the hills the men had crossed earlier.

Fargo motioned for Billy and McNally to continue talking as he stood up. He eased the Colt from its holster on his hip as he moved silently toward the brush. Barely breathing, he stopped and listened. Most men wouldn't have heard the faint sounds made by someone sneaking up on the camp, but the Trailsman did.

Billy and McNally kept up their conversation as if nothing was wrong, although to Fargo's ears the words sounded a little forced and strained. They were normal enough to fool the man skulking toward the camp, however. He kept coming until he was right on the other side of a bush from Fargo, who stood there silent and invisible in the darkness.

Fargo's eyes had adjusted enough so that he could vaguely make out the figure of the lurker. When he saw the man lift something that appeared to be a rifle, Fargo knew it was time to make his move.

His free hand shot out, reaching through the brush, and his aim was unerring. His hand caught hold of the stranger's collar, and then the muscles of his arms and shoulders bunched with power as he heaved the startled man through the brush and into the camp.

The lurker was taken completely by surprise, and the violence of the throw spilled him off his feet. He rolled on the ground between Billy and McNally. As the stranger came to a stop, Fargo stepped out into the open and leveled his Colt at the man. He had eared back the revolver's hammer, and his finger was on the trigger, ready to fire.

"Don't move," Fargo warned, "or I'll blow a hole through you, hombre."

# 7

"Don't shoot!" a familiar voice yelped.

"Charley!" Billy said. "What the hell!"

Fargo grimaced in disgust as he holstered his Colt. "You damned near caused me to kill you, son," he said. "That would've made me mighty upset."

"I'm sorry, Mr. Fargo," Charley gulped as he lay there trying to keep his hands raised despite his prone position. "Can I, uh, get up now?"

Fargo reached down, clasped the youngster's right wrist, and hauled Charley to his feet seemingly effortlessly. "Followed us all day, did you?" he asked.

Sheepishly, Charley nodded. "Yeah. I hope you're not too mad at me. I just wanted to come along and help you find Echo. I thought a few times that I wasn't gonna be able to keep up, but I just kept riding and every so often I'd spot the three of you up ahead."

Fargo didn't say it because he didn't want to encourage the boy, but he thought that Charley had done an excellent job of trailing them, especially in going undetected as long as he had. Fargo's instincts had told him that somebody was back there, but he hadn't caught even a glimpse of the youngster. Charley had some natural talent for this sort of work.

Fargo wished the boy hadn't used that talent on this particular chore, though. Now he was forced to choose between sending Charley back home on his own—and not knowing whether the boy would actually go—or letting him come along as he and Billy and Joseph McNally closed in on the kidnappers, which could easily turn out to be mighty dangerous. Neither choice was very appealing to Fargo.

"You're gonna just have to turn around and go back," Billy told Charley. "This is no place for you."

"Aw, Billy—" Charley began.

McNally interrupted him by saying, "When I was a young man and followed Osceola into battle against the white man's army, many brave Seminole youths no older than this boy fought with us. Our children are born with courage and honor flowing in their veins."

"See, Billy?" Charley said. "Mr. McNally wants me to come along."

"I know you are a devoted friend to my daughter, Charley," the old Seminole said. "And it is a long way back home."

Charley turned to Fargo. "What about you, Mr. Fargo? What do you think?"

"I think you should have stayed put on the farm like Billy and I told you to," Fargo said. "But since you didn't . . . it might be better to have you around so that we can keep an eye on you and try to make sure you don't get into too much trouble. One thing, though . . . you're going to have to do what you're told, right away and without arguing."

"I can do that!" Charley agreed excitedly. He turned to Billy again. "What do you say, Billy? Mr. Fargo and Mr. McNally don't mind if I stay. You'll let me, won't you?"

Billy frowned and didn't say anything for a moment. Charley shifted worriedly from foot to foot. Finally Billy nodded and said, "All right, but I'm tellin' you right now, I don't like it. From here on out, you obey orders, understand?"

"You bet I do! You won't be sorry, Billy!"

"I already am," Billy said with a sigh. "Now, where's your horse?"

Charley pointed into the night. "I left him back there about a quarter of a mile. I didn't want to just ride right in, because I thought you might be mad at me and try to send me back. So I figured I'd sneak up, make sure where you were, and be ready to follow you in the morning."

"How'd you know we were camped here?" Fargo asked. "We don't have a fire, so you couldn't have seen it or smelled any smoke."

"I was close enough to see you stop at the edge of these badlands and I figured you wouldn't try to follow the kidnappers' trail out there until morning. I dropped back a little and dismounted, then left my horse there and came ahead on foot, just to be sure."

Fargo continued to be impressed with the youngster's skills, as well as what seemed to be a canny nature. However, it was at odds with what he had displayed two days earlier when they had first met, after Charley had followed Fargo up that gulch. That day Charley's ability to trail somebody stealthily had seemed to be nonexistent.

"How'd you get to be so good at moving quietly, Charley?" Fargo asked. "A couple of days ago you made almost as much noise as a herd of stampeding buffalo."

Charley looked down at his feet. "Aw, I just . . . I been watchin' you, Mr. Fargo. The way you move around so quiet-like, I mean. I just tried to do things like I thought you might do 'em."

Billy made a strangled noise and said, "You never learned anything from me."

"Sure, I did, Billy."

"What?"

Charley smiled. "How to grin and talk my way out of trouble?"

Then he ducked as Billy took a swipe at his head and Fargo and Joseph McNally chuckled.

Fargo grew more serious as he picked up the rifle Charley had dropped and handed it to the boy. He asked, "Why did you point that rifle at Billy and Mr. McNally just before I grabbed you?"

"I wasn't really pointin' it at them," Charley explained. "I just had it ready in case I was wrong and it wasn't you fellas camped here. I thought it was, but I couldn't be absolutely sure until I heard Billy and Mr. McNally talkin', and by that time it was too late. You'd grabbed hold of me and I was flyin' through the air."

"Caution is a rare thing in one so young," McNally said. "And a good thing, too."

Fargo jerked a thumb over his shoulder. "Come on. Let's go get your horse."

As they headed off through the darkness with Charley obviously trying to emulate Fargo's quiet manner of walking, the youngster said, "I'm glad you and Billy aren't too mad at me. I just want to help Echo."

"I know that. It would have been better if you'd done like we told you and stayed home, but you have to deal with things the way they are, not the way you wish they were. You're here, and we'll make the best of it." Fargo's tone was grim as he added, "But you know this is liable to be dangerous. You could get hurt or even killed."

Charley swallowed hard. "I know. And I won't lie to you, Mr. Fargo. I'm kinda scared. But Echo's always been nice to me. Like I told Billy, she really is sorta like my older sister. If there's any chance I can help her, I want to, no matter what the risks."

"Just do what you're told and pay attention. Maybe we'll all come through this alive," Fargo said.

But he wouldn't have offered very good odds on that. Men who would steal girls and young women and tote them off to God knows what sort of fate wouldn't hesitate to kill anybody who got in their way. . . .

Even though Charley offered to take a turn on watch that night, Fargo could tell that the boy was even more exhausted by the long day in the saddle than the rest of them were. He told Charley to get a good night's sleep and promised him that he could take a turn the next night.

Assuming, of course, that all of them were still alive the next night.

This one passed quietly, and before dawn the next morning the four of them shared a meager breakfast. Having Charley along would force them to stretch their rations a little more than they had planned, but in a land with abundant game and water, that wasn't really a serious consideration.

As soon as it was light enough for them to see where they were going and more importantly to see the tracks left by the kidnappers' horses, they moved out, following the trail down the slope and into the maze of canyons and ridges.

Most of the canyons were deep enough so that they would remain in shadow all day, except for a short time at midday when the sun was directly overhead. This gave the wilderness a feeling of gloom. Nothing good could be hidden in here, thought Fargo.

The trail led them to a fairly wide but shallow stream that curled in and out of canyons as it flowed cold and clear over a rocky bed dotted with sandbars.

Trees lined its banks. Rugged outcroppings of stone jutted from the hillsides above it. In a quiet voice, Fargo told his companions, "Keep your eyes peeled. If we're anywhere near the gang's hideout, there could be lookouts posted up on some of those rocks."

Billy, Charley, and McNally nodded their understanding. Billy and McNally looked tense but calm. Charley was scared—Fargo could see the fear in his eyes—but he was doing his best to control it and not let it affect him. He rode just as steady as the men with him, holding his rifle across the saddle in front of him.

They had penetrated a mile or so into the canyons when Fargo reined in and lifted a hand in a signal for the others to halt. They knew to be quiet without being told to. Fargo sniffed the air. A second earlier he had thought he caught a whiff of smoke, but now he didn't smell it anymore.

There! Suddenly he smelled it again. He sniffed and looked over at Billy, who nodded to signify that he had caught the scent, too. Wood smoke, mixed with the fainter aroma of something cooking. It was unmistakably the smoke from a campfire.

The scent was faint enough so that Fargo knew it came from some distance away. The smoke might waft along these canyons for half a mile, maybe more. But the fact that they were close enough to smell it at all meant that they had to be more cautious than ever now.

Fargo motioned for the others to move back in the direction they had come from. They rode several hundred yards before Fargo stopped and dismounted. Billy, Charley, and McNally followed suit.

"I'm going ahead alone to get the lay of the land," Fargo told them.

"Damn it, Skye," Billy said. "You'd better let me go with you."

Fargo shook his head. "No. If anything happens to me, I want you to be able to come along and get me out of trouble, Billy." He left unsaid the fact that Billy had done just that a couple of days earlier, but the look they exchanged said that neither of them had forgotten about that. "And if I don't come back . . . well, then it'll be up to the three of you to find Echo and those other girls and rescue them."

"Don't talk like that, Mr. Fargo," Charley said. "Nobody can beat the Trailsman!"

"That's where you're wrong," Fargo told him with a smile. "No matter how good you are at anything, there's always somebody better. Don't ever let that stop you from trying to be the best you can be, though."

Fargo shucked the Henry from its saddle sheath. Billy said, "Be careful, Skye."

Fargo nodded and set off on foot. The way the canyon bent back on itself, he hadn't gone very far before he was out of sight of the others.

The snakelike course that the stream had carved out for itself meant that the kidnappers' camp might be only a couple of hundred yards away as the crow flew, but Fargo might have to travel half a mile or more to reach it. He moved with the stealth and patience that long years of adventuring had taught him, sticking to the shadows and the cover of trees and brush as much as he could. He moved so quietly that birds still sang in the trees as he slipped underneath them. A raccoon stood in the water, its masklike face intent as it suddenly reached under the surface and came up with a silver fish wriggling in its paws. An eagle wheeled through the sky overhead.

This was a beautiful land, thought Fargo.

It was a shame that evil men had to bring their ugliness into it.

A short time later he began to hear a low, rumbling, rushing sound. For a moment he couldn't identify it, but then he realized that he knew what it was. The river twisted around a bend up ahead, with a rocky shoulder to the right that blocked Fargo's view. He had begun to smell the smoke even stronger now, though, so he knew he had to be close to the camp. Edging closer to the bend, he pressed his back against the rock and took his hat off. Then he leaned around the corner and risked a quick look.

The stream flowed from a large pond at the base of a cliff about five hundred yards away. Down that cliff and into the pond tumbled the waterfall that made the sound Fargo had heard. A crude trail twisted up the face of the cliff to the right of the waterfall, and at the top of it a boulder perched.

A man sat on a smaller rock next to the boulder. He had a rifle tucked under his arm and was smoking a quirley. He looked back up the canyon, which came to a dead end against the cliff. From that vantage point he had a perfect view and would be able to see anyone approaching the pond and the large log cabin that sat in a curve of the cliff to the left of the pond. Near the cabin was a corral made of peeled poles. Fargo counted seven horses in it, and there were four mules as well.

Fargo knew why the mules were there. A wagon was parked between the cabin and the corral, a wagon of a sort that Fargo had seen before. Sturdy walls enclosed its bed. Each of the walls Fargo could see had a small, barred window built into it. Although he couldn't see the rear of the wagon from where he was, he would have bet that it had a locked door mounted in it.

That was a prison wagon—but there was no prison anywhere around here.

It could be used to carry any sort of prisoners, though, including young women stolen away ruthlessly from their families. As Fargo pulled his head back around the rock, his bearded jaw tightened in anger. What he had just seen gave him a pretty good idea what was going on here.

According to what he had been told, there had been a spate of kidnappings several weeks earlier, then the outrages had stopped for a while. That was because the kidnappers had loaded up their victims in that prison wagon and delivered them to wherever they were going. Then they had come back here to this hideout to start over again, gathering up girls and young women in a sinister harvest. The fact that the wagon was still here meant that the bastards hadn't finished getting their second load together.

And *that* meant that Echo, as well as Billy's sister Wa-nee-sha, were probably still in that cabin, being held prisoner until the kidnappers had enough captives to make it worth their while to load up the wagon and set out again.

It was probably too late to save the first shipment of girls that had left this hellhole, Fargo told himself, but not too late to rescue Echo, Wa-nee-sha, and any other victims who were still here. In order to do that, though, he would have to figure out how he, Billy, Charley, and Joseph McNally could get to the cabin without being seen and free the girls without starting a huge gun battle that would expose them to danger from stray bullets flying around.

The first obstacle was the sentry guarding the approach to the cabin. He would have to be disposed of before they could hope to get close enough to take the kidnappers by surprise. Fargo looked around and then tipped his head back to gaze upward.

No trail led to the top of the ridge that curved

around to form the cliff, but he spotted enough potential handholds and footholds to make him believe that he could climb the rock face. It wouldn't be easy, but he could do it, and if he did then he might be able to work his way around behind the sentry.

With the guard out of the way, Fargo's companions could sneak up the canyon until they were close to the cabin. Then Fargo would have to create some sort of distraction that would lure the kidnappers into the open. When they came out to see what was going on, Billy, McNally, and Charley could get the drop on them. If the confrontation came down to a shoot-out, the prisoners would have the best chance of survival if all the gunplay took place outside.

The plan stood a good chance of working, Fargo decided. And that was all he had ever asked out of life . . . a good chance.

He clapped his hat on and hurried back up the canyon toward the spot where he had left the other three rescuers. Despite his haste, Fargo still moved as quietly as he could. He had spotted only the one guard, but he didn't want to take any chances of giving away their presence.

Billy, Charley, and McNally all raised their rifles instinctively as Fargo came trotting into view, then relaxed as they recognized the Trailsman. "Did you find them?" Billy asked anxiously. "Did you see the prisoners?"

"Was my daughter there?" McNally put in.

"I found the hideout," Fargo told them, "but I didn't see anybody moving around. There are enough horses in the corral, though, that I'm convinced the whole gang is here."

Quickly, he verbally sketched the layout for them and then explained about his plan to take care of the sentry.

"Maybe you ought to let me do that, Skye," Billy suggested. "That would leave you free to lead the attack on the cabin, if it comes to that."

"Or me," Charley offered. "I'm younger, and I can climb real good."

Fargo shook his head. "Billy, no offense, but you've got a bad leg to start with and a stiff arm from that bullet graze. I'm not sure you'd be able to make the climb. And Charley, if you did, you'd have to kill that guard by yourself."

"You think I couldn't do that?"

"I think you're still a boy," Fargo said, not bothering to keep the bluntness from his voice. This was not the time for anything less than straight shooting. "How many men have you killed?"

Charley grimaced. "Well . . . none, when you put it that way."

"That's the only way to put it," Fargo said. He softened his tone a little. "It's not a matter of trust. It's a matter of who's best suited for the job."

"Yeah, I reckon," Charley said with a nod. "We got to do whatever gives us the best chance of rescuin' those prisoners."

Fargo glanced at Joseph McNally. "You're not going to argue with me, too?"

A grim chuckle came from the old Seminole. "I know I could not make a climb such as the one you describe, Mr. Fargo. But I can pull a trigger just fine, if I have to, and kill the men who stole my daughter."

Fargo nodded. "It's all settled, then. And I don't see any point in waiting. Let's move on up the canyon. Lead your horses and be as quiet as you can."

They set off toward the kidnappers' hideout. When they reached the last bend before the long, straight stretch that led to the waterfall, Fargo signaled another halt. He took off his hat and hung it on the

Ovaro's saddle. Then, knowing how well voices could carry in canyons like this, he whispered, "I'll climb up here and work my way around behind the guard. It'll take me a good ten or fifteen minutes. Billy, when that much time has passed, start checking around the bend every minute or so. Be careful about it, though. You don't want that hombre to spot you if I haven't gotten rid of him yet."

Billy nodded and said, a little testily, "I know that, Skye."

"I'll be watching for you," Fargo went on, "and when I see you I'll give you the signal that it's clear. The three of you leave your horses here and work your way as close to the cabin as you can. Stay behind cover as much as possible. I'll draw them out."

"How?" Billy asked.

"I'm thinking about pushing down that boulder. It would make a mighty big crash if it fell."

The other three nodded. "Do we shoot them when they come out of the cabin?" McNally asked.

"Not unless they put up a fight," Fargo said. "Just throw down on them and let them know they're covered. Some of them might stay inside with the prisoners, and we don't want them to panic and start shooting in there. But if they won't surrender . . . well, then, we won't have much choice."

The nods were grim ones this time. All four of them knew that what they planned meant great danger, not only for themselves but also for the prisoners.

But there was no other way that Fargo could see. He left his rifle in the saddle boot. Disposing of the guard would be close, bloody work, best suited for the Arkansas toothpick. A shot would give the game away too soon.

Selecting a handhold, Fargo grasped it and pulled himself up. He wedged a boot toe in a crack in the rock and shifted his grip. Moving slowly and carefully, he ascended the canyon's rocky wall.

Fargo had never liked climbing like this, but his lithely muscular body was well suited for it. When he glanced down a few minutes later he saw that he was already twenty feet above the canyon floor. Thirty or forty more feet would bring him to the top. He kept climbing, making sure that he was secure each time before he shifted a hand or foot.

Even though the air in these shadowy canyons held a hint of coolness in it year-round, a fine sheen of sweat coated Fargo's face by the time he finally pulled himself over the rimrock at the top of the canyon wall. He lay there catching his breath for a moment, then lifted his head and studied the terrain around him.

The ridge top lifted in a slope to his right that was dotted with trees and scrubby bushes. His eyes followed it on around toward the spot where the sentry was posted above the canyon. Fargo recalled that the rock where the man sat was positioned slightly below the level of the rimrock. While the sentry had a perfect view back down the canyon, he wouldn't be able to see as well behind him. If Fargo could be quiet enough in his approach, the man would never see him coming.

Knowing that the others were waiting for him, and depending on him, Fargo came to his feet and began making his way along the rimrock, being careful not to dislodge any stones that might clatter down to the canyon below and alert the sentry that someone was skulking around.

He retreated into the trees and used them for cover as he made his way closer and closer to the guard's position at the top of the trail. The sound of the waterfall was loud now. Fargo dropped to a knee and carefully parted some brush to take a look.

The rimrock's ragged edge was about a dozen feet in front of him. Fargo's instincts had brought him to the right place. He saw the top of the sentry's hat next to the bulge of the boulder that perched at the head of the trail. The trail itself stopped just below the top of the cliff.

Fargo reached down and drew the Arkansas toothpick from the sheath on his calf. He slid almost noiselessly through the brush and edged forward, catfooting closer to the guard. The waterfall so close by made a lot of racket, enough to cover up any small sounds he might make.

He had almost reached the edge when he suddenly realized that he had made a potentially fatal mistake. The sun had risen high enough in the sky to cast a thin, wavering shadow down over the sentry's position. The man must have seen Fargo's shadow move at the same instant Fargo himself noticed it, because he bolted up from the smaller rock where he'd been sitting and whirled around to face the threat behind him, bringing up his rifle as he did so.

In that same shaved heartbeat of time, Fargo leaped off the rimrock, hurtling down at the sentry. He had to stop the man from getting off a shot or letting out a yell, no matter what.

Fargo crashed into the guard and knocked him backward. Both of them sprawled onto the steep trail and began to roll down it toward the canyon floor. The trail's first switchback caught them and stopped their out-of-control tumbling. Luck was the only thing that kept them from going over the edge and falling a good twenty feet to another section of trail below.

Fargo had hold of the rifle barrel with his left hand. He twisted it, wrenching the weapon out of the sentry's grasp. At the same time he drove the knife at the man's body, but the man grabbed Fargo's wrist and with desperate strength held off the blade.

Their faces were only inches apart. Fargo heard the man's gasp of recognition. He knew the freckled features glaring at him, too. This was the redheaded hombre who had tried to kill him three days earlier. Fargo would have liked to ask the man why he'd bushwhacked him, but this was no time for conversation. The redhead's free hand bunched into a fist and slammed against the side of Fargo's head.

Fargo was able to keep his wits about him despite the blow. He still had hold of the guard's rifle, so he rammed the weapon's butt into the man's midsection. The man's grip on Fargo's wrist slipped, but not enough to allow Fargo to plunge the Arkansas toothpick into him. The man opened his mouth to yell, forcing Fargo to drop the rifle and lunge to grab his throat. He choked off the outcry.

In writhing around during their struggle, they had skidded a little farther down the trail. The boulder loomed above them now, and the air was cool in the giant rock's shadow. In grim silence, the two men strained against each other in the life-and-death battle. The outlaw hammered punches against Fargo's head. The Trailsman had no choice but to absorb the punishment as best he could. One hand gripped the knife while the other was locked around the sentry's throat, preventing him from shouting a warning to his friends.

Gradually, Fargo's superior strength began to prevail. He brought the knife closer and closer to his enemy's body as the sentry weakened due to lack of air. The man's punches grew more feeble. Terror gave him renewed strength for a few seconds as he felt the painful bite of the knife as it penetrated his clothes and then his skin, but it didn't last. Fargo heaved and felt the blade slide home. The man's eyes widened in agony as the knife rasped between his ribs and reached his heart.

He seemed to deflate then as the life went out of him. The muscles of his throat relaxed under Fargo's tightly gripping hand. His eyes began to glaze over. Fargo had witnessed enough death, often at close range like this, to know it when he saw it.

Fargo let go of the dead man's throat and put his hand on the trail to push himself up. He pulled the knife free of the man's body and used the corpse's shirt to wipe away the blood that stained the blade. A little shaky from the desperate struggle, Fargo climbed to his feet and looked down at the cabin. No one was in sight, although smoke continued to rise from the stone chimney.

He gazed along the canyon toward the bend where Billy, Charley, and McNally waited. Lifting his left hand above his head, Fargo waved back and forth as he caught a glimpse of movement at the bend.

A moment later he saw Billy emerge from cover and hurry toward the cabin, limping as he dashed behind some brush. Charley came into view, then McNally. All three of them began working their way toward the cabin, being careful about it as Fargo had told them but not wasting any time.

Fargo left the sentry where he had fallen and climbed back to the top of the trail, taking the man's rifle with him. He would probably need it to use as a lever in dislodging that boulder. As soon as he had done that, he would start down the trail so that he could join the others and hopefully help them disarm the kidnappers.

While Billy, Charley, and McNally made their way into position, Fargo studied the massive rock. He had room to get behind it, but not really enough to wedge the rifle in at its base and try to lever it into motion. Instead he wedged himself in with his back against the rimrock and his booted feet against the boulder. The painful muscles in his back reminded him that this was a similar position to the one he'd been in a couple of days earlier when he had worked his way up that fissure in an attempt to escape from the whiskey runners.

Fargo set himself and heaved, bringing all the strength in his legs to bear on the boulder. A lesser man might have despaired as he felt its unyielding mass. Fargo just gritted his teeth and tried again, putting his back and shoulders into it, too.

This time the huge rock shifted, but only a fraction of an inch. Even that much progress was encouraging, though. Fargo let himself slide back down to the ground and stood there catching his breath as he checked on the progress his three allies were making. They were doing a good job of staying behind cover, he saw. If he hadn't known they were there, he might not have been able to spot them as they slipped closer and closer to the cabin. He thought they would be ready by the time he got the rock moving.

Unfortunately, time was something they didn't have as much of as Fargo had hoped, because at that moment a gunshot blasted inside the cabin.

# 8

Fargo tensed as he saw the door of the cabin slam open, hard on the heels of the shot. A figure with thick dark hair tumbling around her shoulders dashed outside. Fargo's heart leaped as he recognized Echo. As she ran, she twisted around and fired back at the cabin.

Thoughts flashed through Fargo's brain. Somehow, Echo had gotten her hands on a gun, and now she was making a break for freedom, just as he and his companions were about to launch their rescue attempt.

Echo had no way of knowing that, however. She had to be thinking that she was seizing her only chance to get away from her captors. But she had placed herself in even more danger, and Fargo expected to hear a shot ring out at any second, a shot that would drop Echo in her tracks and probably end her life.

Instead of firing, a burly man with a dark, tangled beard lunged through the cabin door and gave chase. Echo turned and threw another shot at him, but it missed. The man never broke stride as his long legs carried him after the fleeing young woman. He closed the gap in seconds, and when Echo tried to swing the gun around and fire again, he slapped it aside with one big, brutal paw.

At the same time, his other hand closed on the collar of her shirt and yanked backward. The cloth ripped, allowing one of Echo's breasts to spill from the shirt, but enough of it held together so that she was jerked off her feet. She slumped to the ground.

"Echo!"

The shout came from Joseph McNally, who leaped out from behind the tree where he had hidden and ran toward his daughter. Fargo bit back a curse. He had been hoping that McNally and the others would be coolheaded enough to stay out of sight until the big kidnapper had taken Echo back inside. Then they could go ahead and put their plan into effect.

All bets were off now, though. McNally thrust his rifle toward the kidnapper and yelled, "Get away from her!" Billy and Charley came out into the open, too, and pointed their rifles at the man. Fargo saw the rest of the kidnappers come boiling out of the cabin, hard-faced hombres bristling with guns.

All hell was going to break loose, he realized. There was no way to stop it now.

So he decided that he might as well contribute to it.

He threw himself between the rimrock and the boulder again, drawing his knees up so that he slid down lower as his feet braced against the huge rock. It was now or never, the Trailsman told himself as he threw every iota of his strength into the effort. A grinding rasp came from the boulder.

Fargo rolled the stone.

Once the boulder began to move, its own weight did the rest. It lurched forward, dislodging a shower of dirt and pebbles around its base. Fargo fell to the ground as the boulder tipped over and began to roll. It crashed down onto the trail below, bounced, rolled, fell again, and all the while a roar was building that dwarfed the sound of the waterfall.

Fargo scrambled forward to the edge of the trail and peered over it. He saw everyone below peering upward in astonishment as the boulder came bounding and smashing down the cliff. What seemed to take forever was probably no more than a pair of split seconds, and then the boulder landed in the pool with an earth-shaking crash and a huge splash that threw water high in the air.

While that water still hung in the air, Fargo was already moving. He raced down the trail toward the hideout, Colt in hand. Below, guns began to roar. Through the haze of dust that the boulder had kicked up as it fell, Fargo saw that Billy and Charley had opened fire on the kidnappers to give McNally some cover while the old Seminole dashed forward toward his daughter.

The Colt in Fargo's hand bucked as he added a couple of shots of his own. The bullets from Billy and Charley's guns made the kidnappers duck for cover, but Fargo's lead kept them from retreating into the cabin. He didn't want them getting back in there where they could use the remaining prisoners as hostages.

The burly hombre who had grabbed Echo and torn her shirt stepped forward to meet McNally's rush. He knocked the old man's rifle aside and clubbed McNally in the head with his other fist. McNally slumped to one knee.

Before the kidnapper could press his advantage, Echo leaped on his back from behind and reached around him to claw at his eyes. The man howled in anger and stumbled forward. McNally grabbed him around the knees and jerked his legs out from under him. The kidnapper toppled to the ground, taking Echo with him.

Fargo had almost reached the bottom of the trail.

Flame spurted from a gun muzzle as one of the men fired at him. The bullet whistled past Fargo's ear. He triggered again, and the kidnapper doubled over as the slug punched into his belly.

He was the only kidnapper who had been downed so far, though, and the others were starting to get organized. Their shots drove Billy and Charley into the cover of some trees. Meanwhile, the man who was struggling with Echo and her father got the upper hand as well, backhanding Echo away from him and then sinking a fist deep into McNally's belly as the Seminole tried to get up. Gray-faced and gasping for breath, the old-timer collapsed.

Fargo headed for them, hoping that he might get there quickly enough to turn the tide, but he had to circle the pool to reach them and before he was half-way around it, the kidnapper had hold of Echo again and had started dragging her back toward the cabin.

Fargo turned and went the other way, plunging toward the waterfall. He could see the rocks there and knew the pool was shallow enough he could cross it without having to swim. The water pounded at him as he ducked under the waterfall. He had to be careful not to slip and fall as he leaped from rock to rock.

He burst out of the cascading water and found himself only a few yards from the cabin. Echo was still struggling with the kidnapper, slowing him down. They hadn't reached the door yet. Fargo couldn't risk a shot, not with Echo that close to the man, so he jammed his Colt back in its holster and left his feet in a flying tackle.

He slammed into the kidnapper and knocked him away from Echo. Both men sprawled to the sandy ground in front of the cabin. Fargo rolled over and came up on his knees. As he did so, he saw that the kidnapper was getting up, too. The man lunged at him, swinging a malletlike fist. Fargo ducked his head and took the blow on his shoulder as he hooked a punch of his own into the man's midsection.

Both of them kept punching as they surged to their feet. They wound up toe to toe, slugging away at each other. Fargo gave as good as he got, but the other man was taller and heavier. Fargo knew this was one time he might not be able to match his opponent in sheer power.

But Fargo had a secret weapon on his side. Over the kidnapper's shoulder, he saw Echo snatch up a piece of firewood from a stack next to the cabin wall and step up behind the man, swinging the wood for all she was worth. With her lips drawn back from her teeth in a savage grimace and her breasts heaving where they hung exposed in the torn shirt, she looked like some sort of female warrior, a vengeful Valkyrie bent on destruction. The length of firewood landed on the back of the kidnapper's skull with a horrible crunching crash.

The man's eyes rolled up in their sockets and his knees unhinged. As he pitched forward on his face, Fargo saw that the whole back of his head was caved in. He would never manhandle any more girls or young women.

Fargo grabbed Echo's arm. "Are there any more inside the cabin?" he asked. He wanted to make sure she was all right, but he had more pressing problems right now.

She shook her head. "They all came running out after me," she said. "Skye—"

He interrupted her by shoving her toward the door. "Get in there," he told her. "Close the door and bar it. I've got to go help Billy and Charley and your father."

McNally was still down. Fargo didn't know how

badly he was hurt. That left Billy and Charley to face four men, all of whom had found cover and were now pouring a blistering fire at the two Seminoles. Billy had ducked behind a tree with a trunk barely wide enough to protect his body, while Charley hunkered behind some rocks, unable to move without exposing himself to hostile bullets, every bit as pinned down as Billy was.

That left it up to Fargo.

Echo hesitated outside the cabin. "Skye, let me help—"

"Get inside," he snapped. "That's the best way you can help me now, Echo."

Reluctantly, she stepped into the cabin and swung the door closed. Fargo heard the bar go across it inside. He stepped over to the man Echo had killed and reached down to snag the man's gun from its holster with his left hand. With his right, he drew his own Colt. He started down the canyon toward the rest of the gang. He was behind them, the only one with a real chance to make a dent in them.

One of the men spotted him coming and yelled a warning as he wheeled around. Fargo fired at the same instant as the kidnapper's gun belched flame. The slug whipped past his ear, but his own bullet found its mark, shattering the outlaw's shoulder. The man went down screaming in agony.

Another of the kidnappers turned to bring his gun to bear on Fargo, but as he did so he moved out from the rock that had sheltered him just enough for Billy to draw a bead on him. The former scout fired in the blink of an eye. The bullet punched through the kidnapper's body from behind, throwing him forward as crimson sprayed the exit wound from his chest.

Fargo closed in on one of the other men, both guns bucking and roaring in his hands. The slugs pounded into the kidnapper and sent him jittering across the ground in a bizarre dance of death. As he collapsed in a bloody heap, the remaining kidnapper snapped a shot at Fargo and connected. The bullet barely creased Fargo's left thigh, but it was enough to knock the Trailsman off balance. He slewed half around and fell to a knee. The man who had shot him drew a bead for a killing shot.

Before he could squeeze the trigger, though, Charley popped up from behind the rocks and fired. The youngster's bullet only creased the man's arm, but it was enough to make him cry out and stagger, throwing off his aim as he fired. The next second, Fargo swung his left-hand gun up and triggered a shot that caught the man in his open mouth, blowing a fist-sized hole in the back of the man's skull as the bullet came out. He collapsed like a puppet with its strings cut.

Silence descended on the canyon as the echoes of battle rolled away over the wooded slopes, bouncing back and forth as they gradually diminished. Fargo forced himself to his feet. His thigh throbbed where he had been creased, but his leg worked as he walked forward to check on the man he had shot in the shoulder. That was the only one of the kidnappers who might still be alive.

The glassy, staring eyes and the big puddle of blood in which the man lay told Fargo otherwise. He had bled to death in a matter of moments while the rest of the battle raged around him. The bullet that had broken his shoulder must have nicked an artery as well.

Billy limped toward Fargo while Charley hurried over to help McNally to his feet. "Skye!" Billy called. "Are you all right?"

Fargo looked down at the bloodstained leg of his buckskin trousers and said, "Just a scratch. Reckon I'll be a little gimpy for a while, too."

"Yours will heal up," Billy told him. "And I'm glad. Is Echo . . . ?"

"She seemed to be all right," Fargo said with a nod toward the cabin. "She's in there, probably with your sister and the rest of the gals who have been carried off recently."

Charley and McNally came up, the old-timer leaning heavily on the boy. McNally's face was still gray with pain, but he seemed a little stronger now. "Where is my daughter?" he asked.

"I'll take you to her, Mr. McNally," Billy said. He moved in on the old man's other side, and together the three of them walked toward the cabin.

Someone flung the door open before they got there, and Echo rushed out, followed by four other young women, including a dark-haired beauty about eighteen who threw her arms around Billy's neck and hugged him desperately. That would be his sister Wa-nee-sha, Fargo thought with a smile. The other women clustered around their rescuers, crying in relief and reaction to the ordeal they had been through.

Fargo watched the reunion from a short distance away. He tucked the extra gun behind his belt, then began reloading his Colt. When he was finished with that, he filled up the chambers of the second gun as well. The trouble seemed to be over, but it never hurt to be ready for more.

Echo broke away from the joyous group and came toward him. She had pulled the tatters of her torn shirt across the front of her torso and tied them together so that they covered her breasts again . . . sort of. A lot of smooth, rounded female flesh still showed through the rents in the shirt. As she came up to him, she said anxiously, "Skye, you're hurt."

"It's nothing," he told her. "Is there any whiskey in the cabin?"

Echo grimaced. "Several bottles. Those men—those *animals* would be a better description—stayed half drunk most of the time."

"Then I can use some of it to clean this bullet burn, and it'll be fine." Fargo paused. "Did they hurt you?" His face was bleak as he asked the question. "Or the other girls?"

Echo shook her head. "Whitson—the big one who did this to me—" She gestured at the torn shirt. "He seemed to be the leader, and he said they could get more money for us in Texas if we were pure. That's what they've been doing, you know. They take the girls they kidnap down across the Red River into Texas and sell them to a . . . a place in Gainesville."

"Not anymore they won't," Fargo said as he looked at the bodies sprawled around the canyon.

"I . . . I killed Whitson when I hit him with that firewood, didn't I?"

"You did," Fargo told her honestly. "Probably saved my life and your own, too, when you did it."

"You would have beaten him."

"I wouldn't be so sure about that. Anyway . . ." Fargo smiled. "I think he had it coming."

After a moment, Echo smiled. "I think he did, too," she said. She moved up next to him and slipped an arm around his waist. "Let me help you inside."

Fargo didn't really need her help, but he let her do it anyway. Right now, it felt mighty good to lean on her.

After everything that had happened, it was decided that the group would spend the rest of the day and the night there at the hideout, rather than start back toward the Seminole Nation right away. The five young women who had been held prisoner here had only terrifying memories of their captivity, but they were willing to put up with the place for a while longer to let Fargo and Joseph McNally rest before they set out on the journey home . . . especially once Billy and Charley had loaded the corpses of the kidnappers into the wagon and hauled them away, taking them back down the canyon.

When they got back, bringing the Ovaro and the other horses with them, no one asked what they had done with the bodies, but Billy told Fargo later that he and Charley had found a ravine in which to dump them.

"The scavengers will pick their bones clean," Billy said. "It's nothing more than what they deserve."

Fargo couldn't argue with that. The scheme that the kidnappers had come up with was a particularly horrible one.

"What are we gonna do about the girls they already took down to Texas and sold?" Billy asked as he and Fargo stood beside the pool, which now had the giant boulder forming an island in the center of it. Echo had cleaned and bandaged Fargo's wound, and he could get around now without too much trouble.

"After we get these girls safely back to their families, I'll take a *pasear* down there and see if I can get a line on the others." Fargo shook his head. "I've got to warn you, though, they'll have come in for some rough treatment by now."

"It's not their fault. I reckon their folks will still want them back."

Fargo nodded. "I'll do what I can to make that happen," he vowed.

He spent the rest of the afternoon taking it easy. He was a little worried about McNally, concerned that Whitson's punch might have busted up the old man inside, but by late in the day the Seminole seemed to be getting back to normal except for a large bruise on his belly.

The kidnappers had laid in plenty of supplies. The former captives were able to whip up a good supper for everyone as night fell. After they had eaten, Fargo split up the night into guard shifts. He took the first shift himself.

With the Henry tucked under his arm, he went out into the darkness, taking a stool with him on which to sit so he could stretch out his wounded leg. He placed it near the wall of the cabin, sat down, and leaned back against the logs. The night was quiet except for the small sounds that were always there, and he found them reassuring. After all the violence and terror of the past few days, these moments of peace were even more meaningful.

A while later, the cabin door creaked slightly as it opened and then closed. Fargo turned his head to look in that direction and saw a figure coming toward him. Enough starlight filtered down into the canyon for him to recognize Echo.

"Thought you'd be asleep by now," Fargo commented quietly as she came up to him.

"I can't seem to doze off," she said. "I feel . . . dirty somehow, Skye. Even though those men didn't really do anything to me, they had their hands all over me, pawing me. Whitson and that redheaded one, Jernigan, were the worst." She paused. "Jernigan talked about you. He said the next time he got you in his sights he would kill you, for sure."

"He didn't have much luck with that," Fargo said with a grim smile. "Did he ever say anything about why he bushwhacked me in the first place, the day I rode into these parts and first met you?"

Echo stood beside him, her hand resting on his shoulder. "Actually, he did," she said. "He was scouting for more women they could steal when he spotted you. He recognized you right away, he said, because you'd ruined the plans of a gang he used to ride with, up in Kansas. He had a grudge against you for that, but mainly he just didn't want you anywhere around down here, for fear you'd get mixed up in all the kidnapping they'd been doing. He didn't even know that Billy had sent for you, and yet he was scared of you."

Fargo chuckled. "I've said all along that having a reputation sometimes gets a man into more trouble than it's worth."

"Well, you can't do anything about it now. You're the Trailsman, and you always will be."

Fargo nodded. "I reckon so." He looked up at her. "You'd better go back and try again to get some sleep."

"Not just yet," Echo said. "I was looking at that waterfall, and I wonder if washing off underneath it would make me feel less dirty."

"It might," Fargo allowed. "And I'm right here to keep an eye on you while you're doing it."

"I'd like that." She had put on a different shirt, throwing the one Whitson had torn into the fire, and now her fingers lifted to the buttons and began deftly unfastening them. She shrugged out of the garment, revealing her high, proud breasts. Fargo's eyes had adjusted well enough to the dim starlight so that he could see the dark nipples crowning the firm globes.

After taking off her boots, Echo unfastened her trousers as well and slid them down over her lush hips. When she stepped out of them she stood before Fargo totally nude. She lifted her hands and ran her fingers through her hair. The movement lifted her breasts and made them bob slightly. Fargo watched in profound appreciation.

Echo walked to the pool and waded into it. Fargo enjoyed the rear view almost as much as he did the one from the front. Echo circled around to the waterfall and stepped into the edge of the cascading stream. The water twisted down her naked body in rivulets, almost as if it were caressing her. She plunged her head into the waterfall and let it soak her hair, which hung in sleek, raven black wings over her shoulders. The starlight struck silvery highlights off her wet flesh. Fargo thought she was one of the most beautiful women he had ever seen.

After washing her hair, Echo began running her hands over her body. She cupped her breasts, squeezing and molding them together. Fargo felt his pulse pounding harder in his head, and his manhood began to harden as he watched. Echo continued washing under the waterfall, but those ablutions involved a lot of stroking and caressing, too. She bent over to run her hands down her thighs, then turned so that Fargo could see her cup the cheeks of her bottom and massage and separate them. She turned again as both hands trailed through the triangle of thick dark hair at the juncture of her thighs and then stole between her legs. She gasped and tipped her head back as her fingers worked their magic.

Fargo knew, of course, that she was putting on a show for him, as well as entertaining herself at the same time, and he thoroughly enjoyed it. Echo's hips began to pump back and forth as her fingers flew faster. Fargo leaned forward, watching avidly as she lifted herself higher and higher and finally brought herself to a climax that had her breasts heaving. A low groan escaped from her lips as she shuddered. Then her head fell forward again as she stood there for a long moment trying to catch her breath and the waterfall showered around her.

At last she waded out of the pool and came toward Fargo, her steps slightly shaky as she did so. She bent over him, her hand going to his groin to caress the hard pole through his buckskins. "Let me take care of this for you," she murmured.

Fargo stood up long enough for her to unfasten his trousers and lower them, then he sat down on the stool again and leaned back against the cabin wall as she knelt between his knees. His iron-hard shaft jutted up and seemed to lengthen and harden even more as she stroked it with both hands.

After a few minutes of that exquisite torture, Echo raised the stakes even more by leaning forward and pressing her lips to the head of Fargo's manhood. She slid her lips all the way down the underside of the shaft to the base, then slowly traversed back up to the tip. As if that weren't enough to send the blood boiling through Fargo's veins, she then retraced the journey, only this time with her tongue. Pleasure throbbed all through Fargo's being.

At last Echo opened her mouth and took Fargo inside, wrapping the warm, wet heat around him. Even though he closed his eyes and rested his head against the wall behind him, a part of his brain remained alert. No matter how much he enjoyed what she was doing to him, he hadn't forgotten that he was standing guard over the cabin. He trusted his senses, as well as those of the stallion. The Ovaro would let him know if anyone came around who shouldn't be there.

Other than that, Fargo gave himself over completely to the experience and luxuriated in the sensations Echo sent rippling through him. He felt his climax building and didn't try to hold it back. From the way Echo began sucking harder on his throbbing length, she didn't want him to hold back his release. Fargo's jaw tightened as he let go and allowed his culmination to sweep over him. She swallowed his juices eagerly.

Fargo slumped against the wall as his muscles inevitably relaxed following that peak. Echo's tongue circled his shaft as it softened. When it slipped out of her mouth, she gave it an affectionate squeeze.

"You're a magnificent man, Skye Fargo," she whispered. "I cannot thank you enough for what you've done for me."

Fargo frowned. "This wasn't just out of gratitude, was it? Because if it was, that wasn't necessary."

She laughed softly. "What happened tonight happened because I wanted so badly to experience it. Otherwise I just would have said thank you."

"Well . . . that's all right, then." Fargo took hold of her arms and drew her up so that he cradled her on his lap. Echo was a good-sized girl, but Fargo held her easily in his muscular arms. They kissed and caressed each other, basking in the afterglow of their pleasure.

Finally Echo slipped out of his embrace, picked up her clothes, and began to get dressed. "I think I can sleep now," she said.

"Good," Fargo told her as he stood up and fastened his trousers. "You need your rest. It's a long ride back home. We'll be doing good to make it tomorrow without having to spend a night on the trail."

"If we do have to camp out, maybe you and I can find a moment or two alone. . . ."

"We can hope," Fargo said with a laugh.

He stood there with the Henry tucked under his arm and watched as Echo slipped back into the cabin. He hoped she didn't wake any of the others. He wasn't ashamed of what they had done, but as a gentleman, he believed in the concept of discretion. . . .

A sudden sharp nicker from the Ovaro made him turn toward the corral. The other horses shifted restlessly. Could be a coyote sniffing around, thought Fargo. He was about to go check it out when something else caught his attention—the scrape of boot leather on rock.

He was wheeling toward the sound when flame suddenly lanced out of the darkness, accompanied by the roar of a gun. What felt like a giant fist smashed into Fargo's head. He knew he was falling but couldn't do anything about it, and then he felt the cold shock of water closing around him.

That sensation was the last thing he knew.

# 9

Fargo choked and sputtered, and that brought him out of the darkness that threatened to claim him for all eternity. Each cough sent a sledgehammer of pain crashing through his head, but at the same time he savored that agony because it proved he was still alive.

Water streamed over his face. He ducked his head and tried to shield it with his arms. His fingers rasped against stone. He pulled himself upward, feeling the tug of his soaked buckskins as he did so. The easy thing would have been to slip back under the surface, to let the watery embrace wrap itself around him, but Fargo fought against that temptation. He clambered over the rocks until he was completely out of the water.

Darkness still surrounded him, along with a rushing roar. Cold, wet spray coated his face. Gradually, he came to realize that he was under the waterfall at the head of the canyon, lying on the rocks in the narrow space behind the cascade. How he had gotten there, he didn't know. The last things he remembered were a flash of light and a smashing blow to his head. . . .

Somebody had taken a shot at him, he realized as his stunned brain began to function again. He forced his muscles to work and lifted a hand to his head, to the center of the pain. Above his right ear, his fingers found a small, sticky lump where a slug had barely grazed him.

That leaden kiss had been enough to knock him out and send him tumbling into the pool at the base of the waterfall. He wasn't sure how he had gotten all the way around here behind the falling stream. Even though he'd been unconscious, his instinct for survival must have fought to keep him from going under and he had floated or crawled over here.

*Echo!* Memories of the beautiful young woman surged up in Fargo's mind. She had just gone into the cabin, where everyone else was sleeping. Who the hell had taken that shot at him? Everybody was accounted for, and anyway, none of them would have any reason to try to ventilate him.

Fargo pushed himself up on his elbows and looked around. He spotted a flickering orange glow through the falling water, and the realization of what it was sent shock waves jolting along his nerves and through his muscles.

*The cabin was on fire!*

Without even realizing that he had climbed to his feet, Fargo found himself stumbling through the torrent and then out into the open air. Water splashed around his feet as he staggered toward the blazing structure. Heat from the flames washed over him, forcing him to stop before he could get too close. He lifted an arm to shield his face, just as he had when he came to in the water.

"Echo!" he shouted, lifting his voice to be heard over the fierce crackling of the flames. "Echo! Billy! Charley!"

"Mr. Fargo! Over here! Mr. Fargo!"

Fargo turned toward the sound of the familiar voice. "Charley! Where are you?"

After what seemed like a long time but was probably only seconds, he finally focused on a shape near
the corral. He realized it was Charley. The youngster
waved both arms over his head.

"Mr. Fargo! Help!"

Fargo hurried toward him. Pain still throbbed inside
Fargo's skull, but his steps were steadier now and he
was able to use his iron will to force the pain into the
back of his mind. He saw two dark shapes lying on
the ground near Charley's feet and feared the worst.

Charley clutched at Fargo's arms as Fargo came up
to the boy. "It's Billy and Mr. McNally," Charley said.
"They're hurt!"

"Where are Echo and the other girls?" Fargo asked.
He glanced back toward the burning cabin, afraid that
Charley was going to tell him the girls were inside
that inferno.

Instead, Charley said, "They're gone! He made
them get in the wagon and took 'em with him!"

"All of them? Echo, too?"

Charley's head bobbed in a nod. "Yeah. Billy and
Mr. McNally tried to stop him, but . . . but he shot
them!"

Fargo gripped the boy's shoulders. "Who?"

"The man . . . I don't know where he came
from. . . . I'd never seen him before . . . but Billy
called him Rafferty!"

Shock stiffened Fargo's muscles as he heard that
name. He had believed that Rafferty was dead under
tons of rock and dirt after the exploding whiskey barrels caused that overhanging bluff above the Canadian
River to collapse.

What Charley said next sent ice along Fargo's veins.
"I . . . I never saw anybody who looked like him, Mr.
Fargo! It was like his whole face had been burned off,
but he was still alive somehow!"

So Rafferty had been caught in the fire as the whiskey burned, but he must have managed to crawl through the flames and get out from under the bluff just before it came down. Maybe he was the only one of the whiskey runners who had survived that catastrophe. Bent on revenge, driven by hatred that enabled him to keep moving in spite of his injuries, he must have been trailing Fargo and Billy ever since, waiting for a chance to wreak his vengeance on them.

"You can tell me later exactly what happened," Fargo said to Charley. "Right now we'd better see how bad Billy and Mr. McNally are hurt."

The light from the burning cabin was enough for Fargo to see the bloodstain on McNally's shirt when he rolled the old Seminole onto his back. Fargo ripped the shirt open and rested a hand on McNally's chest, which rose and fell steadily. The old-timer was alive, and when Fargo tore the shirt even more, he saw that a bullet had knocked a hunk out of McNally's side but didn't seem to have penetrated his body. McNally had passed out from shock and loss of blood, but he ought to pull through.

Billy was in worse shape, Fargo saw immediately when he moved over to check on his old friend. The entire front of Billy's shirt was sodden with blood.

Incredibly, Billy was still alive, too. In fact, his eyelids fluttered and he let out a groan as Fargo moved the blood-sticky shirt aside and saw the worst. Billy had at least two bullet holes in his stomach. He was gut-shot, the sort of wound from which no one recovered. At least he had lost enough blood so that he couldn't last much longer, and in its own grim way, that was merciful. Sometimes men injured like this took agonizing hours to die.

"Sk-Skye . . ." Billy whispered.

"Right here," Fargo told him. "You just rest easy, Billy. You'll be fine."

"All the things . . . you can do . . . better'n me . . . lyin' was never one of 'em, Skye . . ."

Fargo didn't respond to that. He leaned over Billy and said, "Charley told me it was Rafferty."

"Y-yeah. . . . Don't know how the son of a bitch . . . is still alive. . . . Did he . . . did he hurt the girls?"

"He took them with him," Fargo said.

"Damn!" Billy lifted a hand and clutched feebly at Fargo's arm. "You got to . . . go after him . . . get 'em back . . ."

"I will," Fargo promised. "You can rest easy about that, Billy."

Billy's eyes closed and a long sigh came from him, and Fargo thought he was gone. But a second later he murmured, "Knew I could . . . count on you . . . Skye." A moment passed, and then Billy whispered, "Skye . . . you know how . . . I got my name?"

"You mean your real name?"

"No . . . Billy Buzzard."

Fargo shook his head. "I don't reckon I do. Folks were already calling you that when I first met you."

"One of the soldiers . . . gave me the name . . . 'cause I was so good at findin' the enemy . . . said I was always circlin' around . . . followin' death . . . like a buzzard . . . what he didn't know . . . was that death was . . . followin' me. . . ."

This time when Billy's head sagged back, the rattling breath that came from his throat was unmistakable. Death followed everybody, Fargo thought, from the moment they took their first breath as babies. The trick was in staying ahead of it as long as you could.

But it had caught up to Billy Buzzard at last.

From behind Fargo, Charley said, "Is . . . is he . . . ?"

"Yeah," Fargo said, "he's gone."

"Mr. McNally's awake now. I helped him sit up."

Fargo came to his feet and turned around. He saw that McNally now leaned against one of the corral poles. The old Seminole's face was drawn and haggard in the firelight, but his eyes glittered with anger as he looked up at Fargo.

"My daughter has been taken prisoner again," he said.

"I know," Fargo told him. "But I'm going to get her back. Rafferty put all the girls in that wagon, and he won't be able to move very fast with it. It won't take me long to catch up to him."

"Take Charley with you," McNally said.

Fargo frowned. "I don't know if that's a good idea. You're going to need help—"

McNally shook his head. "Bandage my wound, and I will be fine. I can take Billy back to his mother and father. You and Charley bring back their daughter, and mine."

"Are you sure about that?"

McNally nodded.

"All right, then," Fargo said, reaching a decision. "Charley, you're coming with me. But first we need to tend to Mr. McNally."

Normally, Fargo wouldn't take anybody as young as Charley along with him on a dangerous mission, but Charley had handled himself well so far and had in fact saved Fargo's life during the gunfight with the kidnappers. After being nicked a couple of times by bullets, Fargo thought it might be a good idea to have someone backing his play when he went after Rafferty.

He tore a strip off McNally's shirt and wet it in the pool, then used it to clean away the blood around the wound in the old Seminole's side. Fargo was able to confirm that the wound was a shallow one.

"I'd feel better if we had some whiskey to clean it with," he commented as he sat back on his heels.

"Use gunpowder," McNally suggested.

Fargo frowned. "That's a mighty painful way to do it."

"I know, but I am an old man. If the wound festers, I might not survive."

"There is that to consider," Fargo admitted. "If you're sure."

"Go ahead," McNally told him.

Fargo used the Arkansas toothpick to pry open a couple of cartridges and sprinkled the gunpowder in the wound in McNally's side. Then, since the lucifers he carried in his pocket were a sodden, useless lump, he got a piece of flint from his saddlebags and knelt next to the old man, holding the knife.

"Hang on," Fargo said. McNally just nodded again.

Fargo struck the blade against the flint as he held them close to McNally's side. Sparks flew, and one of them landed in the wound. The gunpowder ignited with a flash.

McNally threw his head back, the cords in his neck standing out as he gritted his teeth against the pain. Smoke curled up from the wound, bringing with it the smell of burned powder and burned flesh.

"We'll tie some clean rags over that," Fargo said. "You ought to be able to make it back to the farm. Billy's mother can look after you once you get there." He hesitated. "One thing, though. You can't take Billy's body back there. It would take too long. We need to bury him here."

McNally sighed. "I know. I wish that were not true, but it is. Do what you must."

Fargo turned his head to look at Charley. "See if you can find a shovel."

Charley had no luck in that, so finally they had to

use a broken branch to scoop out a shallow grave. Charley did most of the work, and as he did, he filled Fargo in on what had happened.

"There was a shot outside that woke everybody up. Billy and Mr. McNally and I ran outside to see what was going on, and Mr. McNally got hit next. I went to help him, and while I was doing that this man came out of nowhere and threw a burning torch in the cabin. That's when Billy called his name, and they shot at each other." Charley gulped. "Billy missed. Rafferty didn't. I slid under the bottom rail into the corral and pulled Mr. McNally inside with me while the girls came runnin' out of the cabin after it started to burn. Rafferty made 'em get in the wagon. Echo tried to fight him, and he knocked her down and then slung her in there himself. He locked the door so they couldn't get out."

Fargo wasn't surprised that Echo had put up a fight. She wasn't one to surrender to anything or anybody . . . unless she wanted to.

"I was gonna take a shot at him, but then Billy got up somehow and tried to fight again, and he was between me and Rafferty. That's when Rafferty shot him again. Billy fell where he could see me in the corral, and he told me to hold my fire. He said Rafferty probably thought he had killed all of us, and to let him go. Billy whispered for me to find you and go after Rafferty later. He said you weren't dead. He said . . ." Charley stopped and wiped the back of his hand across his nose as tears rolled down his cheeks. "He said that no rotten bastard like Rafferty could kill the Trailsman, that you were still around somewhere and would save Echo and the other girls. I'm sorry, Mr. Fargo, but I did what he said. I let Rafferty think that me and Mr. McNally were dead."

"You did the right thing," Fargo told him. "If you'd

put up a fight, Rafferty would have just killed you and Mr. McNally both. This way we've still got a chance to go after him."

"Who is he, Mr. Fargo? Why's he doin' this?"

Fargo hesitated. With Billy dead, there was no need to go into detail about the whiskey-running scheme. He said, "Rafferty is an old enemy of Billy's. He was with those outlaws we got in a fight with the other day, and I reckon he's been following us ever since, waiting for a chance to get even."

"How'd he get burned so bad?"

"Now that I don't know," Fargo lied. Billy had been wrong about that; he could lie when he had to. He just didn't like it much.

When they had the grave as deep as they were going to get it, they wrapped Billy's body in a blanket from his bedroll and carried it over to the hole. They lowered him as gently as possible. Joseph McNally walked stiffly over to the grave and lifted his voice in a chant. Fargo didn't speak any Seminole, but he knew a prayer when he heard one, so he sent one of his own up as well, a prayer for the soul of Billy Buzzard, no saint, surely, but in the end a man with more good in him than bad.

That was all they could do for Billy, except pile some large rocks on the grave once Charley had used his hands to shovel the dirt back into the hole. "Somebody ought to come back here sometime and put up a marker," Charley said as he straightened from that chore.

"That would be a good job for you," Fargo told him. "Maybe you could bring the rest of his family back here, too, so they can say good-bye to him."

Charley swallowed hard. "I'll do that, Mr. Fargo," he said. "I surely will."

Fargo didn't doubt it. Charley had the makings of a good man . . . if he lived long enough to get there.

That bastard Rafferty might have something to say about that when they caught up to him.

Fargo was anxious to get started after Rafferty, but he knew better than to rush. He used a wet rag to clean the wound on his own head, wincing a little as he swabbed dried blood away from the tender lump.

"You sure got a goose egg there, Mr. Fargo," Charley told him. The roof of the cabin and the walls had collapsed, causing the fire to die down, but enough flames still burned to light up this end of the blind canyon.

"Yeah, it feels like a mule kicked me," Fargo agreed. "I'd like to lie down and sleep for about a week, but in this life, we don't always get to do what we want to do. Mr. McNally's going to rest here until morning, but you and I can start after Rafferty tonight. With that wagon, he's got to follow the canyon until it lifts back up out of here. We'll go that far and then wait until dawn. We ought to be able to pick up his trail then."

"You reckon he's gonna hurt Echo and Wa-nee-sha and those other girls?" Charley asked worriedly.

Fargo shook his head. "I just don't know, Charley. When a fella's half crazed like Rafferty is, there's just no telling what he might do."

After making sure that McNally had plenty of supplies for his trip back home, Fargo and Charley saddled their horses. They fastened lead ropes to two of the kidnappers' mounts. Fargo didn't expect this chase to turn out to be a long one, but if it did, it might come in handy if he and Charley had extra horses so they could switch out riding them. Having fresh mounts available increased a man's speed on the trail, Fargo explained to the youngster.

Then, after shaking hands with McNally, Fargo and Charley mounted up and rode away from the cabin, heading down the canyon by the light of the stars and a thin crescent moon. Earlier tonight those stars had been shining down on Echo's beautifully nude body as she stood there with the waterfall cascading around her. Fargo had trouble believing that only a few hours had passed since that idyllic moment.

Just went to show you how changeable life could be, he thought.

As they followed the twists and turns of the canyon, Fargo kept an eye on their flanks to make sure there were no trails where the wagon could have gotten up to the ridges on either side. He didn't recall any such places, but he wanted to be sure Rafferty didn't slip away from them.

The canyon kept funneling the wagon in a generally southward direction, toward Texas. Fargo wasn't sure exactly how far it was from these badlands to the Red River, which formed the boundary between Indian Territory and the Lone Star State. He hoped to catch up with the wagon before Rafferty reached Texas, but in the long run, that didn't really matter. If he didn't, Fargo would just cross the Red and go on into Texas after the bastard. He would keep going as long as it took, even if it meant crossing the Rio Grande into Mexico. Fargo didn't believe the chase would last anywhere near that long, though.

"I sure hope he doesn't hurt Echo or Wa-nee-sha or any of the other girls," Charley said.

"So do I," Fargo agreed. "But either way, Rafferty's a dead man when I catch up to him."

"You're not going to give him a chance to surrender?"

"You ever hear tell of a rattlesnake surrendering and giving up his fangs, Charley?" Fargo asked.

"Well . . . no, I don't reckon I have."

Fargo nodded. "We won't have to worry about that where Rafferty's concerned, either."

Fargo estimated that the hour was well after midnight by the time he and Charley reached the trail that climbed up out of the canyon to the surrounding plains and rolling hills. They reined in there.

"We'll have to wait here a couple of hours," Fargo said. "By then it might be light enough for us to pick up the wagon's trail. We can't afford to start off on a wild-goose chase. That would just cost us time."

"That makes sense," Charley said, "but it sure is hard to wait, knowin' that Echo and Wa-nee-sha are out there somewhere with Rafferty. I sure hope he don't hurt 'em."

"You and me both, Charley." Fargo didn't mention the very real worry that they might find the wagon with all the prisoners still inside, slaughtered. Driven mad by pain and bloodlust, Rafferty was liable to do anything. . . .

The time passed interminably slowly, but at last the sky in the east began to turn gray with the approach of dawn. Fargo wasn't sure how long it had been since he'd slept. Being knocked unconscious when that bullet grazed him didn't count. He shoved his weariness aside, though. He could keep going for as long as he needed to.

Kneeling where the canyon emerged onto the prairie, Fargo studied the ground in the grayish light. He saw where the wagon wheels had pushed down the grass, and as he followed the marks, leading the Ovaro and one of the spare horses, he spotted more sign, droppings from the mule team pulling the wagon. The trail headed due south.

"He's making a run for the Red River," Fargo said. "Maybe he thinks he'll be safe once he gets south of it." Fargo grunted. "He's wrong."

They mounted up and moved out, following the wagon's trail toward Texas. Fargo didn't move too fast, because he didn't want to risk losing the trail. But even proceeding cautiously like this, he figured they were making better time than the wagon, which was heavy to start with and was now loaded down with prisoners.

The sun rose to their left, peeking over the horizon at first as it turned the sky pink and gold and orange, then bursting into flame as it ascended into the heavens. The air turned hotter almost right away. Even though it was still spring and the blistering days of summer were a couple of months off, it could get mighty warm in this part of the country at this time of year.

Along with the heat, though, the sun brought plenty of light, and Fargo and Charley were able to move faster now. They urged their mounts into a ground-eating lope that covered the miles. The terrain alternated between wooded hills and grassy flatlands, neither of which slowed the pursuit. The grim-faced riders kept moving all morning, stopping only when it was necessary to rest the horses. They gnawed on jerky and sipped from their canteens while they were in the saddle.

They were at the crest of a long rise when Charley exclaimed, "Holy cow! I think I see the wagon up yonder, Mr. Fargo!"

The Trailsman's keen eyes had spotted the wagon in the distance a second before Charley did, but since it was at least a mile ahead of them, Fargo thought it was pretty impressive that Charley had seen it anyway.

"Yes, that's it," he said without slowing the stallion. "This is where things get tricky."

Charley glanced over at him and frowned. "What do you mean?"

"If Rafferty sees us coming, he's liable to stop the wagon and hurt the girls, or at least try to use them as hostages against us. Even crazy like he is, he probably realizes that he can't outrun us in that wagon."

"Then what are we gonna do?"

Fargo thought about it for a moment, then said, "We're going to let him come to us."

# 10

Now that they had spotted the wagon, Fargo and Charley increased their speed. They didn't follow the vehicle directly, however. Fargo waved for Charley to follow him as he veered to the west, toward some trees.

"Handling the team like that, he probably didn't spot us yet," Fargo explained, raising his voice so that Charley could hear him over the pounding hoofbeats. "We don't want him to see us. We're going to get in front of him and set up an ambush."

"That way we can get the drop on him and he won't have time to hurt the girls," Charley guessed.

"Right! Come on!"

They rode hard, angling through the trees and then turning so that they paralleled Rafferty's course several hundred yards to the east. Fargo tried to keep as many trees and ridges between them and their quarry as he could, as he and Charley flashed over the landscape. When he judged that they must have passed the wagon and drawn a considerable distance ahead of it, Fargo turned east again. Now they had to find a suitable place to stop Rafferty.

"What's that?" Charley asked, waving a hand at a long line of trees and bluffs to the south.

"That'll be the Red River," Fargo said. "Those hills on the other side are in Texas."

"I've never been there," Charley said, and Fargo heard a familiar wanderlust in the youngster's voice. He knew what it was because he had heard it in his own voice at times in the past. Charley wouldn't be content to stay on the farm the rest of his life. One of these days he would have to go see the elephant for himself.

They came into a valley that narrowed down and pointed like an arrow to the river. A mile or so back up the valley, the wagon trundled toward them. About a hundred yards south of their position, a trail dropped rather steeply toward the river. Fargo figured there was a ford down there that was Rafferty's destination.

Fargo wheeled the stallion. "Head for those rocks over there, just above the river," he told Charley. "That's where we'll stop Rafferty."

Some good-sized boulders clustered on either side of the trail, overlooking the Red River. Fargo and Charley reined in and led the horses into a nearby stand of trees where they would be hidden. They tied the reins to saplings, pulled their rifles from the saddle sheaths, and hurried back to the rocks.

"Here he comes," Charley said excitedly. "He'll be here in a few minutes!"

"Keep your head down," Fargo told him. "We don't want him to spot us now." He added a bit of advice. "Might be a good idea to take a few deep breaths, too. If you're too worked up, it's liable to throw off your aim if you need to shoot. Being accurate starts with being calm."

"I'll try," Charley said, "but it ain't gonna be easy."

He drew in the deep breaths and released them slowly, and after a few minutes Fargo could tell that the youngster had settled down quite a bit.

"I'm ready," Charley announced quietly.

Fargo smiled. "You know, I think you are. When Rafferty gets here, I'll step out and stop him. You cover me."

"All right," Charley said with a nod. His hands gripped his rifle tightly, but not too tightly.

Fargo had the Henry ready. The wagon was close enough now that he could hear its wheels creaking. Holding the rifle slanted across his chest, he stepped out from behind the boulders. He snapped the Henry to his shoulder as he drew a bead on the man perched on the driver's seat, a slouch hat pulled down in front of his face.

Only it wasn't a man at all, Fargo realized a split second later as he recognized Echo's wide, terrified eyes peering at him over the gag that was tied in her mouth. Her arms and legs were tied, too, and she had been lashed onto the seat so that she had to remain upright.

A figure clinging to the rear of the wagon leaned out, thrust a pistol toward Fargo, and fired. With the cunning of a wild animal, Rafferty had figured that there might be a trap waiting for him at the river, and he had taken precautions against it. The gun in his hand roared as Fargo tried to shift his aim.

Rafferty's bullet struck the Henry's barrel and glanced off, missing the Trailsman but tearing the rifle out of his fingers. Fargo felt the painful impact of the bullet all the way up both arms. He didn't let that stop him as he reached for his Colt.

But before Fargo could get off a shot, Rafferty scrambled atop the wagon like a grotesquely scarred ape and flung himself toward Echo. Fargo couldn't risk hitting her, so he held his fire as Rafferty looped his gun arm around Echo's neck and used his other hand to grab the reins and slap them against the back of the mules. Fargo hoped that the startled animals would balk and refuse to move, as mules sometimes did, but they lunged forward instead, barreling right toward him.

At the last second, Fargo threw himself aside to avoid being trampled and then run over by the wheels. As he rolled out of the way, he shouted, "Hold your fire, Charley! Hold your fire!"

Charley must have already figured out that he couldn't chance a shot, either, because he ran into the trail and waved his rifle at the mules, shouting as he tried to get them to stop. The spooked creatures didn't slow down, though, and Charley was forced to leap aside, too.

Fargo was already on his feet again by the time the wagon passed him, and he flung himself into the air, reaching out with his free hand for the padlock that hung on the door. His fingers closed around it, and he felt his feet jerked off the ground. The door had a small lip along the bottom of it. He heaved with all his strength and pulled himself up so that he could rest the toes of both feet on that lip.

Through the small, barred window in the door, he saw figures in the gloom inside the wagon and knew they had to be Wa-nee-sha and the other captives. "Hang on!" Fargo told them, then holstered his gun and reached up for the roof of the wagon with that hand.

The vehicle swayed and jolted in the ruts of the trail as it started down toward the river. Fargo caught a glimpse of the stream as he climbed onto the top of the wagon, clutching tightly at small handholds as he was almost thrown off several times. The Red River lived up to its name. The stream was about sixty feet wide and the same rusty color as the bluffs that bordered it on each bank.

Fargo didn't have time to draw his gun as he

149

reached the wagon's roof. Rafferty twisted around on the seat and blazed away at him. Fargo had only a glimpse of the man's hideously burned face before he had to throw himself forward so the slugs passed over his head. A second later he crashed into Rafferty and grabbed the man's wrist to force the gun to the side, away from him.

They wrestled desperately, each man knowing that this was a life-and-death struggle. Echo was right against Fargo's side, hampering his efforts a little, but she couldn't move because of the way she was hogtied.

Rafferty flailed away at Fargo with his free hand while trying to bring his gun barrel back to bear on the Trailsman. Only inches separated their faces now, and Fargo saw that Rafferty's injuries were even worse than Charley had described. The flesh had melted away from the man's face, so that the white of bone showed through in several places. Rafferty's nose was nothing but a charred lump, his mouth a lipless slit. But his eyes seemed unharmed, and they blazed with a fierce insanity. He lowered his head and butted it into Fargo's face. Fargo felt the ooze of rotting flesh on his skin and his stomach twisted with revulsion.

The mules stampeded on down the slope, and when they reached the bottom they didn't slow down. They missed the ford, though, and hit the soft bottom of the river that was almost as bad as quicksand. The wagon slewed out of control as Fargo and Rafferty battled atop it, and suddenly Fargo felt empty air under him as the two men were thrown clear. A few yards away, the wagon toppled over into the river with a huge splash.

Fargo never let go of Rafferty's gun hand, even when they hit the surface themselves. They went under, and Fargo tried not to swallow too much of the rusty water. He got his right hand on Rafferty's neck as they rolled over and over. The fingers of his left hand remained clamped around the wrist of Rafferty's gun hand.

They came to a stop in a relatively shallow area. Fargo jerked his head up and gulped down air as it broke the surface. At the same time, he bore down hard with his right hand, holding Rafferty's head under. Rafferty thrashed wildly but couldn't break free of Fargo's grip as the Trailsman forced his head deeper and deeper.

The river was shallow enough here that Fargo could dimly see Rafferty's ruined face through the murky water. It was a blurred, distorted picture, and it became more so as Fargo pressed down and the sandy bottom began to swallow Rafferty's head. Mud flowed over his hideous features. Rafferty bucked and heaved but couldn't dislodge Fargo.

The madman's struggles grew more and more feeble. Fargo didn't know if it was his choking grip on Rafferty's throat or the mud of the river bottom sucking him down that was killing Rafferty, and Fargo didn't care. All that mattered was that only one of them would come out of the Red River alive, and Fargo intended for it to be him.

Rafferty stopped fighting and went limp. Fargo held him down for another minute just to be sure the man was really dead this time. Then he let go of Rafferty and heaved himself to his feet, fighting against the mud. As he looked around, he realized that he might have made a terrible mistake.

The wagon lay on its side, mostly submerged in the water. And Fargo couldn't see Echo anywhere.

He remembered that she had been tied to the seat. He broke into a run toward the overturned vehicle and started swimming when the water got too deep for his feet to reach the bottom. From the corner of his eye he saw Charley running down the trail toward the river.

Fargo paused and waved a hand at the rear of the wagon as he shouted, "Charley! Bust the lock on the door! Get the girls out of there!" With every second that passed, more water had to be flowing into the enclosed wagon through the barred windows.

Fargo resumed swimming and went under as he reached the front of the wagon. The thrashing hooves of the mules had stirred up the mud so that he couldn't see anything now, but he felt his way along until he touched cloth. Fighting the urge to panic, he ran his hands along the body that he couldn't see until he came to the rope that fastened Echo to the wagon. Fargo reached down to pull the Arkansas toothpick from its sheath and began sawing through the rope.

The fibers were tough and thick, but the knife's razor-sharp blade sliced through them quickly. Quickly enough, Fargo hoped. As soon as the rope parted, he threw his arms around Echo's limp form and kicked his way to the surface. He swam hard for the bank, towing her with him.

Her face was still and white, and as he laid her out on the sandy bank he couldn't tell if she was breathing or not. He ripped the gag out of her mouth, turned her over, and pumped hard on her back to force the water out of her lungs.

Suddenly she coughed and spewed water from her mouth. Fargo rolled her over again and helped her sit up as she continued to cough and retch. Under the circumstances those were wonderful sounds, because they meant that she was alive.

Frenzied splashing made Fargo glance around. He saw Charley come to the surface. The boy cried, "Mr. Fargo! Mr. Fargo! I got the lock busted, but the door's stuck! It won't open!"

The water must have made the wood swell and bind, Fargo thought. Echo was only semiconscious, but he had no choice except to ease her back down onto the sand and plunge into the river again. He reached Charley's side, and they both took deep breaths and ducked under the water.

Working by feel again, Fargo found the window in the door and grasped the edge of it, between the bars. He pulled hard on it and felt the door move slightly. Grabbing Charley, he put the youngster's hands in the window and then felt along the door until he came to the edge of it. He was able to work his fingers into the crack that his previous effort had opened. Gritting his teeth, Fargo heaved on the door while Charley pulled at the window.

The door popped open abruptly, making both of them fall back. Fargo recovered quickly and reached into the wagon. He felt cloth, grabbed it, and tugged. Someone swam past him and headed for the surface. Fargo went into the wagon and guided the girls out one by one as he found them.

A little air remained at what was now the top of the enclosure. It had been the wagon's left side before it turned over. Fargo figured the girls had been floating up there, breathing what little air was left, because they were all conscious and able to help themselves to a certain extent.

Within a couple of minutes, the wagon was empty. Fargo felt all around inside it to be sure, then headed for the surface himself. His lungs felt like they were about to burst. Air had never tasted so good as it did when he finally emerged from the rusty river.

Gasping for breath, Fargo floundered out of the water onto the bank. Echo was conscious and sitting up now. She mustered a weak smile for Fargo as he dropped to the reddish sand beside her.

"Is it . . . is it really over?" she managed to ask.

"Rafferty's . . . dead," Fargo said. "It's over."

"Who was he? What . . . what happened, Skye? Where are Billy and my father?"

"Your father's all right," Fargo told her.

Echo's eyes widened. "Billy . . . ?"

Fargo shook his head solemnly.

Then he put his arm around Echo's shoulders and drew her against him as she began to cry. The other girls were sobbing, too, because they had heard Echo's question and seen Fargo's response. Charley tried to comfort them as best he could.

Yes, this ordeal was over, Fargo thought.

But the sorrow it had caused would last for a long time.

Six weeks later, Fargo stood beside the pool in the canyon with Echo and Charley. At their back was the burned rubble of the cabin where Echo, Wa-nee-sha, and the other girls had been held prisoner. Back along the canyon, near the marker that Fargo and Charley had put up earlier for Billy, the members of his family stood in silent mourning, along with now-recovered Joseph McNally. The group had made the pilgrimage here to say their final farewells to their wayward son, brother, and friend.

In the time since the showdown with Rafferty at the Red River, Fargo had rested and healed for a few days, then set off for Texas to try to track down the rest of the kidnapped girls who had been taken there. He had been partially successful, finding six of the eight in whorehouses in Gainesville, Dallas, and Fort Worth. He had convinced the owners of the houses to let them return to their families, although probably nothing could ever blot away the shame they felt. To Fargo's way of thinking, what had happened to them hadn't been their fault by any stretch of the imagination, and he hoped that someday they would be able to find some peace and go on with their lives.

The other two girls had vanished where not even a Trailsman could find them. Fargo suspected that they were dead, victims of the gréed of evil men.

"What are you going to do now, Mr. Fargo?" Charley asked. He was standing straighter and prouder these days, Fargo noticed, and he figured he ought to stop thinking of Charley as a boy and start thinking of him as a young man.

"What I always do, I reckon," Fargo replied. "Drift along until I find something interesting."

"You could stay with us, you know," Echo said. "You may not be Seminole, but you will always be welcome in the Seminole Nation."

"I appreciate that," Fargo said with a smile, "but I've never been one to let grass grow under my feet."

Echo sighed. "That's what I was afraid you'd say, Skye. I'll be sorry to see you go. But you'll come back someday, won't you?"

"Nobody knows the trails they'll wind up following, I reckon." Fargo turned to Charley and clapped a hand on the young man's shoulder. "I'll be counting on you to look after things around home."

Charley nodded. "I will. I won't let you down, Mr. Fargo."

Until the day came that Charley had to hit the trail, too, thought Fargo. When that happened, his adopted family would be sorry to see him go.

But there were some calls that had to be answered,

thought Fargo. The lure of the unknown, the siren song of the wild frontier . . .

He knew because he heard that song himself, and always would.

---

**LOOKING FORWARD!**
**The following is the opening**
**section of the next novel in the exciting**
***Trailsman* series from Signet:**

**THE TRAILSMAN #326**
**SILVER MOUNTAIN SLAUGHTER**

---

*Arizona, 1861—in the heat of the desert,*
*amid the cacti and the sagebrush, only one*
*thing burns hotter than the sun above—the*
*Trailsman's fury.*

Winter in the high country had been hard, about as
hard as the Trailsman could remember. He'd spent
the better part of it high up in the California Rockies
in an old trapper's cabin. When he wasn't huddled
against the bone-numbing cold and its accompanying
biting wind, he'd split most of his time between gathering what wood he could find that was fit to feed his
fire, and trying to persuade his horse, the Ovaro, not
to climb directly into it to keep warm.

At winter's end, the tall man and his trusty black-
and-white paint stallion had emerged relatively safe

and sound, if a little on the gaunt side, and had headed southeast—a path which took them down toward the Arizona Territory and its promise of sunshine and warmth.

Well, he was sure as hell reaping that promise now, he thought in exasperation as he rode the flat, desolate stretch of desert between Phoenix and Tucson. It had been eighty degrees when he woke at just past dawn, and now, at midmorning, he was sweating up a storm and cursing his buckskins. He would have been smarter to make himself a buckskin loincloth!

Suddenly, he reined the Ovaro to a halt, slithered down out of the saddle, and began to tug off his shirt. When it finally loosed its damp hold on his skin and he peeled it off, overhead, the breeze tickling his skin felt like a miracle.

"Better," he hissed between clenched teeth as he cinched his shirt across the back of his saddle, then secured it with the tie-down latigos.

He knew it was stupid to ride without a shirt this time of year, but right at the moment, the pain of a future sunburn was nothing compared to the here-and-now hellish steam bath of riding inside that leather shirt.

He swung up onto the Ovaro and nudged the stud into a slow jog, the breeze tickling his long-suffering skin. *Yes,* he thought, *much better.*

And then he noticed it.

Just a dot on the horizon, a dot growing larger and separating into tiny black figures as he drew nearer. *Bandidos?* Pilgrims? A million possibilities tumbled through his mind as he rode closer. Not hostile Indians, he decided early on. At least, as soon as it became apparent that one of the objects ahead was a buck-board, which was definitely not an Apache affectation.

But something about the rig—and the folks travel-ing with it—seemed somehow wrong. For one thing, the fellow in the driver's seat wore a tall stovepipe hat with a turkey feather sprouting from its hatband. He also wore a bright yellow vest, the sort in which you might expect to see some New Orleans cardsharp attired. But not an Arizona pilgrim, or a miner, or a cattle or horse rancher. It was the wrong sort of picture.

Beside the odd duck driving the team sat what looked like a young girl. Maybe twenty or so, Fargo thought. But that was probably just wishful thinking. It had been a few months since he'd set his eyes on a girl worth looking at.

"Don't start getting yourself bothered," he mut-tered so that only the Ovaro heard. "She's probably some old Hopi squaw."

Still, he pushed the Ovaro into a speedier jog.

Although it seemed like forever, he caught up with them in no time, and the rig's driver didn't seem sur-prised to see him. "Took you a while," the old man said, turning slightly in his seat. Protruding from the outlandish hat was a scant series of long, white wisps that the Trailsman hadn't seen from afar, and the man seemed to have only a quarter of his original comple-ment of teeth. Those that remained were stained by tobacco.

The girl didn't look at either one of them. She just kept the same posture she'd held since he first made her out—slumped forward, eyes on her hands in her lap. He couldn't see her face, but he took some comfort in the fact that her hands didn't look old and gnarled.

Fargo turned his attention back to the wagon's driver. "You a pilgrim?" he asked, more as an excuse to keep pace with the rig than out of any real curiosity.

The old man jutted a skeletal hand out toward him. "Franklin Q. Stubbins, at yer service."

The Trailsman took it and gave it a shake. "Skye Fargo's my name," he said. "Most folks know me as the Trailsman."

"I will, too, then," said Franklin Q. Stubbins, and then he broke out into a quick but loud bray of laughter. The girl beside him didn't shift so much as half an inch.

"What you doing out here in the nowhere, Mr. Stubbins?" Fargo asked. "You on your way to Tucson?"

Again, the old man broke out into that peculiar bray of laughter. "Mebbe, mebbe," he replied. "We'll see how the water holds out."

The Trailsman's brow wrinkled. Just what did the crazy old coot mean by that? He looked over at the girl again. She had cringed down into herself at Stubbins's last comment, and Fargo was beginning to wonder how they had paired up. And if she was as crazy as Stubbins was. She'd have to be either crazy or desperate to share a buckboard seat with him all the way down to Tucson.

So he simply nodded, as if the old man's comment about the water made perfect sense to him, and asked, "Where do you and your daughter plan to bide? I've heard good things about the Wigwam Hotel."

His little stab at finding out about the girl bore fruit sooner than he'd hoped, because Stubbins immediately replied, "Oh, she ain't my daughter, no, not by a long shot. Been a few years since I had the itch so

160

bad I'd scratch it with a squaw." And then came that laugh again.

"Not your wife, either?" Fargo asked.

"Hell, no," Stubbins said. And then he punched the girl in the arm hard enough to nearly knock her from her perch. "Speak up, gal," he said. "Tell the Trailsman here your name!"

Fargo had nearly jumped from his horse to the buckboard's seat when Stubbins struck the girl, but she suddenly wheeled toward him and he forgot all his good intentions.

She was striking. Her features bore the high cheekbones and faraway—but at the same time, intense—look of an Indian, yet her skin was not the copper or latigo color he'd expected. It was pale, almost milky, and blue eyes burned out of her face, burned him to his core.

"I am Kathleen Dugan," she said in a monotone, then turned her face from him once again.

It was a good thing she had, as the shock of her had almost made him lose his scat. While he pulled himself together again, Stubbins added, "Her pa was from County Cork, and her ma was an Apache squaw. They was neighbors to me. Her ma died and her pa went broke, and he sold her into servitude. Got her papers right here." He patted his vest pocket. "I'm havin' me some financial wear and tear of late, and that's why we're headed for Tucson. Gonna try and sell her."

Fargo barely let the last words come out of Stubbins's mouth before he asked, far too eagerly, "How much?" He knew the Tucson he was used to was chock-full of rowdies and scofflaws who'd think nothing off buying the girl, then renting her out for a nickel an hour. Or worse. All that he wanted at this moment was to permanently sever the bond between Stubbins and the fair Kathleen Dugan. The girl wouldn't even look at him for more than a second, and had said no more than four words to him in the entirety of their acquaintance. If you could call it that.

Thoughtfully, Stubbins scratched his chin between thumb and forefinger. "I'd hoped to get me a biddin' war goin'," he said. "Hoped to get enough to buy me a couple of weanling hogs and a calf. And some grain. And mayhap a fair saddle horse." He kept on scratching his chin and gazed out over the horizon.

Fargo felt himself reaching for his pocket. Well, dammit, there were some things a man just had to do.

He opened his coin purse and rooted around for the two double eagles he had put away last fall, in case of dire emergency. This was one, all right.

"Forty bucks," he said, holding the money out so that Stubbins could see but not reach it. "Final offer."

Stubbins hesitated and Fargo let him stew for a moment before he started to draw his hand back.

"Hold on there, son!" Stubbins blurted out. "I'm thinkin'!"

Fargo let his hand drop to rest on his leg while the buckboard and the Ovaro moved them down through the desert. If the girl had any feelings about the transaction or her impending sale, she didn't make them known. She hadn't even looked at him, not once, save when she'd said her name at Stubbins's command.

Fargo asked, "Can she say anything besides her name? You ain't tryin' to gyp me with a one-trick pony, are you?" In truth, he had sort of been hoping that she'd be a fair conversationalist, seeing as they were going to ride down to Tucson together.

He figured to cut her free once they got there, but talking was the only thing he figured to be able to do with her till they made town. And that was another sixty miles or so.

Suddenly, he was having conflicting thoughts about her, and her freedom, and without thinking, began to draw his money-holding hand back toward his pocket.

Stubbins must have had great peripheral vision, because he suddenly snapped, "She can recite the whole Bible, almost. And I reckon forty dollars would do it, son."

This time, the laugh that followed was less a bray than a cackle. It plucked at Fargo's spine like icy fingers.

It had about the same effect on the girl, because he saw her curl in on herself. Suddenly he didn't have any doubts anymore.

He reined in the Ovaro, and Stubbins held his mule. Fargo, finding the transaction more and more distasteful with each passing second, once again held the coins out toward the old geezer, stopping an inch short of where the old man could grab them. Stubbins made a face and opened his mouth, but Fargo beat him to the punch. "You said she's got transfer papers?" he asked.

"Sure, sure, she does," Stubbins croaked, and dug a grimy sheet, folded several ways, from his pocket. He waved it at Fargo. "Got 'em right here."

"Well, sign her over," Fargo said, and leaned forward to let Stubbins take the money. He sat his horse while Stubbins dug out his pencil, then made his mark on the tired sheet.

Stubbins folded the paper back the way it had been while he said, "Get down, girl. You been bought." As he handed the paper up to Fargo, the girl jackrabbited off the other side of the wagon and about ten feet away from the buckboard. She stood there, head bent toward the ground, her arms circling her torso, her hair hanging in her eyes.

Fargo took the sheet and unfolded it, quickly scanning the spidery scrawl before he refolded it and stuck it into his back pocket. The girl was his. At least, on paper. She continued to stare at her feet.

He had expected more. Maybe a thank-you.

Stubbins tossed a ratty carpetbag to the ground, then clucked to his mule and continued on his way without another word to either of them, leaving Fargo and the girl to stare at each other. Or not. He was staring at her, but she was still focused on her shoes, which he'd just noticed were grimy moccasins.

He took her in. At least, as much as she was letting him see. She wore a faded red calico skirt that fell over long, slim legs and softly belled hips, and her blouse was white and very loose, in the Mexican peasant style.

Stubbins and his rig had nearly disappeared from sight before Fargo had the presence of mind to say, "Miss? Miss, you want to climb up behind? It's a long way to Tucson, and I don't want you travelin' on foot."

Finally, she looked up at him, turned that beautiful face toward him. In a voice that was soft but devoid of expression, she said, "Screw you, white dog."

Fargo didn't know how to react, so he just stared at her as if someone from afar was remotely operating her mouth and voice. But she'd said it nonetheless, and eventually he had to say the word that had balled up in his mouth. Which, unfortunately, was "Huh?"

"You heard me," came her reply.

She wasn't looking at him any longer, but he could guess her expression by the tone of her voice, which had grown decidedly more hostile since Stubbins had moved on down the road.

By now, he and his rig were little more than a dark, smudgy speck in the sun-blasted distance.

Fargo didn't answer her, just kept on staring at Stubbins's tiny, disappearing form to the south. But finally he said, "Get up," and reined the Ovaro in front of her.

She looked up at him, hate suddenly pasted across that beautiful, fair face, and grunted an ugly sound.

Fargo didn't like the tone of it, not one bit, but he slid his boot from the stirrup and said, "Now."

Apparently he said it sternly enough that it had effect, because suddenly she slipped up behind his saddle and planted her fanny firmly on the Ovaro's croup.

Fargo was about to welcome her aboard when, from behind him, came her words.

"Well? Didn't you want to take me someplace? Get on with it! Or are we just going to sit here all day?"

Jaw clenched, he gave the Ovaro a little knee, and as the horse moved them forward, muttered, "Buddy, the next time you see me wantin' to do some good, or to do the right thing, just kick me right square in my bleedin' backside."

*No other series packs this much heat!*

# THE TRAILSMAN

**Follow the trail of the gun-slinging heroes of
Penguin's Action Westerns at
penguin.com/actionwesterns**

National Bestselling Author
# RALPH COMPTON